Whispers from the Intoxicating Abyss

Lee Clark Zumpe

Whispers from the Intoxicating Abyss
Lee Clark Zumpe

All rights reserved. No part of this book may be reproduced or transmitted in any form or by any means, electronic or mechanical, including photocopying or recording or by any information storage and retrieval systems, without expressed written consent of the author and/or artists.

Whispers from the Intoxicating Abyss is a work of fiction. Names, characters, places, and incidents are products of the author's imagination. Any resemblance to actual events or persons, living or dead, is entirely coincidental.

Story copyrights owned by the author.
Cover illustration by Marcia Borell
Cover design by Laura Givens

First Printing October 2023

Hiraeth Publishing
P.O. Box 1248
Alamogordo, NM 88310
e-mail: hiraethsubs@yahoo.com

Visit www.hiraethsffh.com for online science fiction, fantasy, horror, scifaiku, and more. Stop by our online bookstore at for novels, magazines, anthologies, and collections. **Support the small, independent press...and your First Amendment rights.**

Contents

7   As a Shadow, And Without Hope

48   The Damascus Code

68   Thy Soul to Him Thou Servest

85   Upon an Altar in the Fields

102   Defector

113   Izothaugnol Ascending

128   The Breach

142   What Sorrows May Come

159   Their Prison Ordained in Utter Darkness

Acknowledgments

"As a Shadow, And Without Hope," previously unpublished

"The Damascus Code," published in *Dark Horizons* in 2015

"Thy Soul to Him Thou Servest," published in *Street Magick* in 2015

"Upon an Altar in the Fields," 5published in *Dread Shadows in Paradise* in 2016

"Defector," published in *Tales of the Talisman* in 2012

"Izothaugnol Ascending," published in *Cthulhu Express* in 2006

"The Breach," published in *Horrors Beyond* in 2005

"What Sorrows May Come," published in *Arkham Tales* in 2006

"Their Prison Ordained in Utter Darkness," previously unpublished

To Mama Bear, B-Bear, Wesley (the cat bear) and George (the teddy bear who protected me from all the ancient horrors beneath the bed).

6

As a Shadow, And Without Hope

1.

> The dusk grows deeper, and on silver wings
> The twilight flutters like a weary gull
> Toward some sea-island, lost and beautiful,
> Where a sea-syren sings.
> From *This Is My Hour,* Zoe Akins

Dwight Howell huddled in the haze of self-imposed isolation and alcohol-fueled anguish at a favorite watering hole in the heart of St. Augustine, Fla.

A dodgy tavern favored by a select troupe of outcasts and misanthropes, Ribault's Revenge had maintained a reasonably successful business in one of the city's oldest neighborhoods and boasted a sordid history as turbulent as the community that spawned it. The century-old establishment borrowed its name from the Huguenot captain Jean Ribault who, in 1565, met a grim fate at the hands of Pedro Menéndez de Avilés, Spanish explorer and founder of St. Augustine, the oldest continuously occupied European-established city in the continental United States.

"Last call," said Silas Merry, the tavern's grizzled proprietor, to the half-dozen remnants of the night's callers. Over the years, Merry had grown steadily more portly as his prosperity waxed and waned. Well past 60, he had thin, steel-gray hair; bulging, watery eyes and not quite enough teeth. He wandered over from behind the bar to the secluded booth Howell had colonized five hours earlier. "You've been coddling that apricot peach ale for an hour now, professor."

These days, Ribault's Revenge featured a preposterous pirate theme and served a selection of local microbrewery ales. Beach music and tropical rock wafted through the bar soullessly, the local barflies gorged to the

8

point of queasiness on Jimmy Buffett chestnuts. Merry's poorly executed plan to lure tourists out of mainstream pubs and chain restaurants failed miserably: His longtime clientele – a disheveled and odious lot at best – frightened away most potential patrons.

"I'm not quite a professor," Howell said, forcing a compulsory smile to form on his lips. Word had spread that he had finally managed to earn his bachelor's degree in journalism at Drayton College, a small, private four-year liberal arts school. Howell had been a student for nearly a decade, shifting majors and neglecting studies in an attempt to postpone adulthood. "It's just an undergraduate degree. Hardly worth anything in this economy."

"As if you need to worry about that," Merry said with a wink. It was no secret that Howell had inherited a fortune – though precisely how his parents had earned their wealth no one knew. "Besides, I have to brag about you a little: Far as I know, you're my only regular who's managed to get a diploma – and it's a college one, at that!"

"Hats off to me," Howell said, raising his bottle in a mock toast. He downed the last of it and carefully placed it back on the table amidst concentric rings of condensation. "Too bad no one showed up to celebrate my achievement with me."

"Too bad *she* didn't show up to celebrate, you mean," Merry said, his insight surprisingly keen. He retrieved the empty bottle and wiped away the warm, wet circles with a filthy rag. "Haven't seen your girlfriend in a long time. How's she doing?"

"Wouldn't know."

Howell did know, of course.

Karina Coletti had written him off more than a year ago after accusing him of "lethargy and chronic hesitancy." She chastised him for squandering his 20s, wasting his intellect and treating his education and their relationship like it was a game without consequences. Publicly, he shrugged off their breakup as if it had no impact. Privately, it had devastated him – and it had given him the impetus to buckle down and complete the last courses he needed to earn his degree.

He had even managed to find a job as a stringer for a local newspaper, though he certainly did not need the income.

Coletti, meanwhile, had transferred from Drayon College to the city's better-known learning institution, Flagler College. She had one more semester to go before completing her bachelor's in business administration. Howell had not seen her in six months, but he knew from mutual friends that she had already been hired by the nonprofit outfit where she had been interning when they were dating.

"Well, you probably shouldn't have brought her here if you were serious," Merry said, trying to lighten the mood. "This ain't really a good place to take a date. This is a good place to get over the one that got away. Or at least drink until you forget her. Speaking of which – did you want another beer?"

"Wouldn't mind a diet soda for the road," Howell said, glancing at the clock on the wall. It was nearly 2 a.m. As usual, he would be shambling down the city's narrow, brick-paved streets skirting ancient shadows, his senses dreamily tangled in half-imagined phantasms echoed nightly by ghost tour guides. "Hope it isn't raining out there."

Unlike New England's oldest cities, St. Augustine – nearly four and half centuries old – never flaunted its antiquity, though it certainly had learned to profit from it.

A popular tourist destination, visitors had been coming to see the Spanish Colonial buildings and 19th century Victorian architecture since the early 1900s. Running through the heart of the old city, St. George Street had become a focal point, its somber city gate providing a distinguishing link to its remarkable past. The street's historic homes dated back to various colonial epochs.

Yet, over the years, some of these structures had been rebuilt or refurbished. Modern gift shops sat next to 150-year-old dwellings. Paved parking lots covered 18th

century market squares. The building blocks that originally gave rise to early defensive lines had been repurposed to build colonist's homes which had in turn been reclaimed to construct businesses, schools and churches.

In St. Augustine, the very old often seemed indistinguishable from the relatively recent.

Howell had hiked the one-mile route between Ribault's Revenge and his modest apartment near the Drayon College campus hundreds of times over the last 10 years. He followed Charlotte Street north, crossing King Street and passing by Harry's Seafood Bar and Grille where the late-night clean-up crew industriously hauled the last bags of garbage out through the courtyard and heaved them into the dumpster in the alley. He passed a row of stately bed-and-breakfasts, including one whose widow's walk played host to a forlorn spirit according to legend.

Turning onto Hypolita Street, the sounds of sporadic traffic along Menendez Avenida gradually faded into silence. The black May night saw the east coast of Florida blanketed in clouds from a distant tropical wave sweeping northward from the Bahamas. Steady onshore winds kept the night unnaturally cool. Crossing over St. George Street, Howell found himself completely alone at an intersection which – by day – was swarming with foot traffic.

Hypolita Street was another narrow little thoroughfare made categorically claustrophobic – particularly at night – by overhanging balconies and high garden walls with lattice gates. A handful of old coquina shellstone houses, moss-roofed, lingered in this stretch, owned by families whose ancestors had been in residence during British rule from 1763 to 1783.

Turning onto Cordova Street, Howell drifted lazily down the moss-hung lane, glimpsing palms and palmettos, magnolias and myrtles and Moorish-styled hand-inlaid mosaic fountains in shadow-draped lawns. Usually, this section of the route proved the most peaceful: hushed backyard gardens and vacant alleyways dispelled the tumult of daylight hours generating a static harmony capable of laying bare centuries of muted whispers from spectral migrants.

On this night, the wraithlike figure Howell encountered near the gates of the Tolomato Cemetery was no ghost.

Glimpsing him from a distance, he inferred from the man's emaciated figure and ragged, loose-fitting clothes that he was one of the city's destitute, compelled to roam the streets by night scavenging for food. St. Augustine's homeless population had multiplied tenfold during the recent recession. City council members acknowledged the crisis but, with tax revenues dwindling, possessed no resources to mount an effective response.

Instead of seeking solutions to the problem, politicians passed ordinances banning panhandling. Many business owners took steps to push the homeless out of areas frequented by tourists, labeling them "an embarrassment" and a "social stigma."

Howell instinctively ducked beneath an arched alcove in a wall surrounding a Spanish-style home, hoping to avoid contact with the individual. He felt neither sympathy nor loathing for the man: He simply had no wish to interact with him.

While he watched and waited, two peculiar figures wearing odd-looking, long-flowing hooded robes – the kind of attire one might expect priests to don for ceremonial purposes – emerged from the cemetery gates, barked indiscernible invectives and scuffled briefly with the homeless man before forcibly leading him back into the graveyard. The confrontation lasted no more than a minute and – though the homeless man's vigorous resistance and muffled pleas for help clearly established his lack of willingness to go quietly – not a single light flickered to life in the windows of adjacent buildings. The twilight itself seemed determined to suppress the incident.

From his hiding place, Howell watched as the three disappeared into the shadows.

Following the brief altercation, static harmony once again settled upon Cordova Street.

Disturbed by the event, Howell scurried past Tolomato Cemetery and hastily completed his journey home.

2.

> Then by the bed-side, where the faded moon
> Made a dim, silver twilight, soft he set
> A table, and, half anguish'd, threw thereon
> A cloth of woven crimson, gold, and jet:
> O for some drowsy Morphean amulet!
> From *The Eve of St. Agnes*, John Keats, 1820

Dwight Howell's cell phone started ringing at 7 a.m. Howell immediately recognized the ringtone: He had assigned David Bowie's "I'm Afraid of Americans" to his boss.

Hoping the caller would be satisfied leaving a voicemail message, he clutched at the vestiges of his uneasy slumber and burrowed beneath the sweat-stained pillows. For three exasperating hours, disquieting dreams had plagued his restless sleep. Though he tried to dismiss it, the incident on Cordova Street had left him shaken.

A minute of precious silence elapsed and then the anxious ringtone returned.

"Hello?" Howell swung his legs over the side of the mattress. The cramped bedroom reeled slightly and a dull ache materialized behind his eyes. "This is Howell."

"Grave desecration overnight, need you to cover it." Joel Nye, the managing editor of the St. Augustine Citizen, lacked people skills when dealing his stringers. A cross between Boo Radley and a rabid grizzly bear, he seldom spoke – but when he did, he did so in a manner that made anyone he addressed feel like they were being verbally mauled. "Investigators are already on scene. No time to waste. Ready for the information?"

"Don't need it," Howell said. "Tolomato Cemetery, Cordova Street."

"You got it. How'd you know?"

"Call it a hunch." His curiosity almost immediately eclipsed any nagging trepidation he might have had. "I'll be there in 15 minutes."

* * *

As city and county police officials squabbled about how best to conduct the investigation, Howell traced the perimeter of the historic cemetery, carefully sidestepping indiscriminately-placed crime-scene tape and searching the crowd of law enforcement officials for a familiar face.

Once the site of Guale Indian village, as far back as the 16th century the land became a burying ground for Indian converts to Christianity as well as former slaves from the Carolinas who had converted to Catholicism. It lay just outside of the dismantled Rosario Line, a defensive embankment forged during the first Spanish period. Residents of this repository for the dead included Minorcan indentured servants and their descendants; the first Bishop of St. Augustine, Augustin Verot; and Jorge Biassou, leader of a Haitian slave uprising in 1791 who became a Spanish general in charge of the black militia in Florida.

"Damn shame, ain't it?" Police spokesperson Sgt. Andy Wilson held a cup of expensive flavored java from a local coffeehouse. As Howell approached, Wilson tucked the remaining crime-scene tape into his belt. "The things kids get into these days," he said, as if he had not been equally mischievous a little more than five years ago. "You'd think they'd have respect for sacred grounds, right?"

"Apparently not," Howell said. Howell and Wilson had developed a decent rapport over the last year, even though the journalist knew that Wilson rarely had the critical details he sought. No one ever managed to get a scoop off of Wilson. "Is that the assumption – bunch of juvenile delinquents caused this damage?"

"Well, it's a working theory."

Howell got as close as he could to the defiled grave. In the ground, he saw a circular hole approximately the diameter of a dinner plate. From what he could tell, its sides were smooth as if it had been excavated with precision equipment.

"How deep is that hole?" Howell started snapping pictures with his camera, but his location behind the crime-scene tape offered no usable images. "And where is the dirt that came out of the ground?"

"The hole is 10 inches across and 7 feet deep," Wilson said, reciting information one of the investigators had fed him within the last 20 minutes. "The displaced soil has not been identified at this time. It is too early to tell if the remains in the grave were disturbed."

"Well, that's something," Howell said. "So, who was buried there, Sherlock?"

"I, um," Wilson said, surprised that no one had given him the name. In fact, Howell knew the cemetery had been closed to burials in 1884 – so, whoever it was, they had been in the ground for more than a century. There had been two additional, unauthorized interments after the closure – the most recent in 1892. "That information isn't available."

"Isn't available?" Howell almost laughed. "Do me a favor," he said, handing Wilson his camera. "Walk over there and snap a few shots of the headstone for me, OK?" Wilson seemed more irritated by the inconvenience than by the potential violation of police procedure. "No one will notice," Howell added, goading him toward momentary insubordination. "They're all busy trying to figure out whose jurisdiction this is."

Fortunately, Sgt. Andy Wilson was highly susceptible to suggestion.

A few minutes later, the camera back in his possession, Howell examined the images. The white marble upright headstone featured a decorative ivy border and an unusual stylized cross at its zenith. The upper half of the cross incorporated a circle which enveloped a small star and crescent moon. The epitaph read:

> *In the hope of blessed immortality here rests the remains of Erastus Luddington, a native of Arkham, Mass., who died at his*

residence in the city of St. Augustine on the 23 of May 1877, aged sixty and four years. Husband of Mary Dolores Luddington. Father to Charles, Ann, Joseph, Henry Eugene and Maria Dolores.

"Any witnesses come forward?" Somehow, Howell dreaded asking the question. He knew he should locate the individual in charge of the investigation – presuming one had been selected – and report his encounter from the previous night. Howell also knew his boss, Joel Nye, hated reporters who became part of the story they were assigned to cover. "Must have been someone in the area last night."

"Too early," Wilson said, rolling his eyes. "Detectives are doing the footwork, knocking on doors. If we're lucky, one of the businesses that backs up to Cordova Street will have surveillance cameras. Maybe one captured some footage."

That revelation quickly displaced Howell's fear of retribution from his editor. If cameras managed to capture images of the vandals, they may have captured images of his trek through the neighborhood in the wee hours of the night, too.

"Better get one of your detectives over here, Sherlock," Howell said grudgingly. "I might have some information for you."

* * *

It took Sgt. Andy Wilson 30 minutes to figure out who was in charge.

It took only five minutes for Dwight Howell to convey his story to St. Johns County Deputy Sheriff Everett Harris. His description of hooded figures escorting a homeless man into the cemetery generated a raised eyebrow and involuntary smirk. Harris thanked him for his input, took his name and contact information and handed him a business card with a request to call if he recalled any additional details.

By the time Howell had coaxed a few more details out of city police officers handling perimeter control, small cliques of area residents gathered along Cordova Street sharing conjecture. Their speculation ranged from the mundane to the supernatural, blaming the sacrilege on everyone from treasure hunters to extraterrestrials.

Howell singled out an isolated neighborhood homeowner wearing curlers and a bathrobe and sipping iced tea from a plastic cup. After showing her his press credentials, he asked her opinion.

"Vagrants, probably," the middle-aged woman said, putting no effort into concealing her revulsion. "This city's overrun with them. Street corners and alleys and libraries by day – parking lots and parks and graveyards by night. I've seen them in Tolomato a hundred times, called the cops and complained. No one ever does anything. The city council should pass a law, round them all up and ship them out of the county."

"Have you ever witnessed them destroying property like this?"

"They live like animals," she continued, ignoring the question. "They should be treated fittingly."

As Howell recorded her remarks in his notebook, he noticed an older man wearing dirty jeans, oversized sneakers and an old army coat shuffling down the opposite side of Cordova Street. He pushed a grocery cart filled with what appeared to be rubbish he had collected from residential trash cans and restaurant waste bins.

The drifter glided by police officers and onlookers without causing a stir, almost as if he traversed the chaotic scene unnoticed.

Howell stood firm as the homeless man swept by him, mesmerized by his bleak expression, his mechanical gait, his arched body buckled by untold calamities. Most of all, though, Howell perceived an awful vacancy in his gaze and – an instant after the man had passed – he wondered if he had imagined the swirling black clouds swarming in his eyes.

3.

> ... there, in a land that knows not age nor winter, midnight, nor autumn, nor noon,

where the silver twilight of summer-dawn is perennial, where youth does not wax spectre-pale and die ...
From *Letters to Dead Authors*, by Andrew Lang, 1886

Dwight Howell could not shake the feeling that he was running late for a class as he walked through the front doors of Drayton College's Marshall Hall.

His first visit to the school since his recent graduation, Howell had set up an impromptu meeting with a favorite professor, hoping to capitalize on their friendship to add flavor to his story on the Tolomato Cemetery incident. He had already emailed a brief sketch of the story to St. Augustine Citizen managing editor Joel Nye – an epigrammatic summation of the details that could be posted on the newspaper's website. The full story, however, would not run until the print editions hit the street the following morning. Howell still had a few hours to go digging in the dirt.

"Excuse me," Howell said, standing in front of a diminutive desk in the school's humanities department office. He recognized the young woman working as clerical support – remembered her from one of his classes. He scolded himself for not knowing her name. "I have an appointment with ..."

"Mr. Butler," she said, looking unenthusiastically at a stack of papers that needed filing. "He's the only professor here," she said. "Everyone took the week off before summer session."

"Right," Howell said. "Mr. Butler."

"He's expecting you," she said. "He had to run over to the library. He said you could wait in his office."

For a moment, Howell considered striking up a conversation with the young woman whose name he could still not recall. She was attractive, rosy-cheeked, blue-eyed and blonde and something about her expression suggested that she was desperate for a distraction. Several years ago, such temptations had been irresistible. He had shelved his playboy demeanor for Karina Coletti. Even though that relationship had crashed and burned, he never quite re-established his knack for captivating women.

Left alone to his thoughts as he waited, Howell found himself dredging up memories of Coletti, replaying the highlights as well as the struggles. Coming from a broken and loveless home, he had no model to follow as their casual college affair blossomed into a much deeper intimacy. For months, he avoided telling her about his inherited wealth, fearful that it would somehow corrupt their bond.

Ultimately, his prosperity did play a role in splitting them apart – but not in the way he had expected. Coletti came to loathe his riches because she felt it made him complacent, purposeless and indifferent. She accused him of being lackadaisical in school and uncommitted in their relationship.

Against all reason, Howell still hoped she might give him a second chance. He had sent her a carefully-worded text message inviting her to join him at Ribault's Revenge the previous evening, to celebrate his graduation.

Coletti neither responded nor appeared.

"When I said you could drop by anytime, I didn't expect to see you quite so soon, Dwight," said Matthew Butler, assistant professor in the humanities department at the school. "You look at home in a college professor's office. Rethinking graduate school?"

"Not yet," Howell said, shaking Butler's hand. "Sorry about bugging you on an off week. I just thought this thing at Tolomato might interest you."

Butler graduated magna cum laude with a bachelor's history from William Whitley College in Tahlequah, N.C. He received both his master's degree and doctorate in history from Tusgagunee University, in north Georgia, where he specialized in 20th century Southern cultural history with an emphasis on Southern religious traditions. At Drayton, he taught Colonial Florida History, American History, World Civilization, Southern Cultural History.

"Well, I was surprised to get your call this morning," Butler said, setting a stack of books on the corner of his desk. "You're right, though, not often I get be quoted in the St. Augustine Citizen talking about grave robbers."

"So, who was Erastus Luddington?" Howell opened his notebook and took out his pen. He placed a small digital recorder on Butler's desk. "Mind if I record this?"

"Certainly not," Butler said. "Well, it so happens Erastus was a well-respected physician – an educated man from an aristocratic family. He served as a Union surgeon in the 121st New York Volunteers. Kept a practice in his hometown – Arkham – as well as in New York City."

"How did he end up in St. Augustine?"

"I found some digitized newspaper articles about him in the library," Butler said, opening a folder filled hazy reproductions. "After the Civil War, he got involved with some carpetbaggers and ended up traveling the Southern states and the territories. He was hawking a cure-all called Essence of Irem. This wasn't the standard snake oil, though. He attracted some very well-to-do customers and he made a fortune."

"So he was a 19th century pharmaceutical company?"

"More or less," Butler said. "In 1872, he settled here and brought his family down from Massachusetts. To give you an idea of how much he was worth at this point, he brought in a team of workers to construct a bluff overlooking the Matanzas River. Then he built a huge mansion on top of that."

"What happened to the house?"

"Couldn't tell you," Butler said. "Probably bulldozed for condos 50 years ago."

"So why would someone want to dig up his grave?"

"To be honest, I'm not sure why he was in Tolomato to begin with." Butler pulled an odd looking old tome out of his stack of books and flipped through the pages. "Look here," Butler said, pointing to a grainy black-and-white picture of a group of men wearing ceremonial cloaks similar to the garments worn by the men Howell had witnessed in the cemetery. "This is from a 1920s book on fraternal orders and magical organizations. They were pretty common back then – private clubs where a town's most well heeled gentlemen could go for a few drinks, to talk shop or ..."

"Dig up graves?" Howell had not mentioned seeing hooded figures in the cemetery to Butler. "Or were they more concerned with bringing about the end of civilization?"

"Not so much," Butler laughed. "That's what today's conspiracy theorists like to suggest, though. Sells more books."

"So, Luddington was a member of this group?" Howell squinted, scanning the faces of the long-dead members of esoteric brotherhood. "The grand wizard even?"

"Front row, third from the left," Butler said. Howell shuddered involuntarily when he looked closely at Luddington's face: His eyes, unlike the others in the photograph, seemed to be occupied by an unearthly silver hue that resonated power and intensity even in this blurred picture. "This is St. Augustine's only known hermetic order, Fraternitas Argenteus Crepusculum, which existed from 1871 to 1898."

"Do you think that interest in this order had something to do with the grave desecration?"

"To be honest, Dwight – not really." Butler closed the book, and Howell felt relieved to be liberated from the trance of Luddington's uncanny gaze. "This kind of thing isn't really common knowledge. It's not like you can Google Luddington and turn up a dozen hits about Fraternitas Argenteus Crepusculum. It does strike me as odd that Luddington was laid to rest in a Catholic cemetery, though. At the time of his death, his involvement in the order would have been common knowledge. It's unlikely he would have been welcomed by the church."

"Well, you did say he was rich," Howell pointed out. "Money has a way of changing people's minds."

"True enough," Butler admitted. "And that's all I have on Erastus. It might be interesting to note in your story that this isn't the first grave desecration at Tolomato, though."

"I found some old newspaper articles online about vandalism at both Tolomato and the Huguenot Cemetery," Howell said. "I do know how to do some research, professor."

"Of course you do," Butler said. "But, I bet you didn't find anything about an incident involving Jean-Jacques Philippe, a self-proclaimed Jamaican-born Haitian houngan."

"Name doesn't ring a bell."

"This was more than a desecration," Butler said. "Someone dug him up during a scheduled cemetery restoration back in the 1990s. The city managed to keep it out of the news since the whole cemetery was cordoned off anyway."

"You're saying someone literally took the remains out of the ground," Howell said. "No, I didn't come across anything about that online."

"They took the body, the coffin and whatever else was down there," Butler said. "This Philippe was no Haitian Vodou priest. He served under Jeannot Bullet during the Haitian Revolution and was known to have ordered his troops to carry out massacres of French civilian populations. We're talking serious, sadistic torture. And any soldier who challenged his command was butchered on the spot to set an example."

"Sounds charming," Howell said, jotting notes. "You sure you want to be quoted on this? If they've been covering this up for all these years, they must have a reason."

"I'm close to retirement, Dwight: They can't really do anything to me now. They called in a few of us as consultants and expected us to be quiet about it. Never signed a piece of paper swearing an oath, though."

"So, what happened with this Philippe guy?"

"After Jeannot was put to death, Philippe disappeared. He turned up in St. Augustine in 1801, claiming to be a freed slave from New Orleans," Bulter said. "An interesting side note is that the one person in St. Augustine who could have identified him, Jorge Biassou, died around the same time Philippe arrived. After converting to Catholicism, Philippe apparently lived a quiet, humble life after that; died in 1842 – and no one ever knew what he had done back in Haiti."

* * *

Howell was in the archives room of Drayton College's library when his cell phone started playing a ring tone he had not heard in more than a year.

Mazzy Star's "Fade Into You" alerted him to Karina Coletti's call.

"Hello," he said, muffling his voice and trying to find the shortest path to the exit. He stuffed his laptop into his backpack and grabbed a sheet of paper off a nearby printer. "Can you hold on a second, I'm in the library."

"I'll wait," Coletti said, and Howell felt a sudden mix of lightheadedness and nausea.

"Sorry," Howell said, reaching the front of the library. Media specialists eyed him maliciously as he dashed by the checkout counter. "I'm doing some research on a story."

"That's OK," Coletti said. "I'm the one who owes you an apology. I didn't get your text message until this morning. I've been so busy at HOST I haven't had a chance to check my phone."

"Oh, don't worry about it," Howell said, hardly wanting to admit his profound disappointment from the previous night. "Although it wasn't much of a celebration without you."

"I'm so proud of you. I didn't even know you were graduating. I would have come to the ceremony."

"I didn't want to bother you with all that," Howell said. He paused, his mind overflowing with prose poetry he had unconsciously prepared for her. "It's good to hear your voice."

"It's good to hear your voice, too," she said. "Look, why don't we get together for lunch or something. Today, my schedule's full but tomorrow would be good. How about some place on the waterfront, on San Castillo Drive."

"What about that Mexican place we used to go to?"

"Two-for-one margaritas: perfect," she said. "It will be so good to catch up with you."

Their conversation remained cordial throughout without either party revealing their deepest sentiments. Howell contained his exhilaration at the prospects of a reunion while Coletti limited her enthusiasm to praising him for finishing his degree. When they had finalized their plans and said their goodbyes, Howell marveled at how speaking to her still seemed so effortlessness and carefree – and at how just the sound of her voice still elated him.

He glanced at the time on his wristwatch before gathering his belongings and heading for the parking lot. Still two hours to deadline: Plenty of time to piece together a strong story about the Tolomato Cemetery grave desecration exploiting the information Assistant Professor Matthew Butler had provided. The sidebar about the 1990s event would surely raise a few eyebrows on the city council.

Tomorrow, he would follow up on one last lead.

In the archives room, Howell had managed to find an old map published by the county tax assessor. The map showed the Luddington estate – found several miles south of St. Augustine on the Matanzas – still existed in the late 1950s. Cross-referencing the archival map to current digital maps, he believed the estate might remain intact, nestled on a strip of land bordering the Matanzas State Forest.

Howell did not notice a small cluster of homeless people milling around the fringes of the parking lot until he reached his car. Three stood listlessly beneath a sweetbay magnolia while two others clambered along a sidewalk, wandering indolently amongst scurrying students. They made no discernible attempt to solicit money from passersby. The world excluded them – they seemed unattached, dislocated from reality.

Though Howell could not see the details of their faces from a distance, he recoiled from the awful blackness he imagined haunting their eyes.

4.

In the ancient room at the oriel dreaming,
Pale as the blooms in her hair; and, wide,
Her robe's rich satin, flung stormily, gleaming,
Like shimmering silver, twilight-dyed.
From *My Lady of Verne*, Madison Cawein, 1898

"Depending on who you ask, HOST stands for 'Helping Outcasts Succeed and Thrive' or 'Helping Others Succeed and Thrive,'" Karina Coletti explained, scanning the lunch menu at Acapulco Mexican Restaurant. "I prefer the latter, personally. I think using 'outcasts' to describe the homeless evokes bad undertones."

"The facility is impressive," Dwight Howell said, trying to keep the conversation neutral while inhibiting the flood of memories he had experienced all day waiting. As they had agreed, he picked her up at the HOST Center of Hope on Dixie Highway south of the city. "I mean, from the outside, it looks like the corporate headquarters for some Fortune 500 company."

"It was all built with donations," Coletti said. "What did I used to get here that I liked so much? Was it the Plato Cancun?"

"That sounds right," Howell said. "What all goes on in that building? It can't all just be for housing the homeless."

"No, not at all," Coletti said. "I mean, we do have about 125 residents at any given moment, staying onsite in small apartments. But HOST is about more than just providing people with temporary shelter. We have job readiness programs, a state-of-the-art medical facility and a modern library with Internet access. HOST is committed to ending homelessness by getting people off the street and finding ways to integrate them into society."

"You've practiced that line a lot, haven't you?" Howell said, immediately regretting it. He had not intended the remark to sound so arrogant. "Don't get me wrong," he added, covering his tracks. "I can see how dedicated you are to this and how rewarding it must be. Frankly, it's inspiring to know there's an organization out there that's making inroads in solving the homeless problem."

"It is rewarding," Coletti said, somewhat taken aback by Howell's genuineness. "But I don't want to monopolize the conversation bragging about HOST. I want to talk about you – what you've been doing, what you're plans are."

"Well," Howell began, realizing his answer had to be concise and enlightening without a hint of aimlessness. Fortunately, he had anticipated the question and had prepared a response. "Right now, I want to put my degree to use working in the field for at least a few years. I'm comfortable at the St. Augustine Citizen but I would consider offers from other daily papers in Florida, particularly in Jacksonville or Orlando. Within five years, I plan to go back for my graduate degree with the intention of teaching at a community college or university."

"Wow," Coletti said, and her emerald eyes echoed her approval. "You are not the Dwight Howell I remember." The link they felt had been irreparably disengaged suddenly seemed capable of restoration. "I read your story about the Tolomato Cemetery this morning. I like the way you incorporated historical aspects. All the local TV news has been doing is rerunning clips of the cops tramping all over the graves and refusing to comment on anything."

The dialogue continued faultlessly for more than an hour. The discussion covered a variety of topics as Howell and Coletti waltzed around an emergent affection that paralleled their former romance. He melted at her every smile, and she implied that she would be willing to reexamine their relationship over time.

"I supposed I'd better be getting back to work," she said, reluctant to end the rendezvous. Their lunch plates long removed from the table, their waiter had been growing impatient for some time, dropping not-so-subtle hints about paying the cashier on the way out the door. "I think I'd better make a quick stop before we go, though."

While Coletti visited the restaurant's restroom, Howell praised himself for having the courage to face her and finding the strength of will to make something of his life. He gazed out the window, sweeping the waterfront from the Bridge of Lions to the massive Castillo de San Marcos. The stronghold stood as the most observable surviving symbol of former Spanish power in Florida. Built between 1672 and 1695, during its 205 years of service the imposing fortress had seen several flags fly over its four bastions, including two periods of Spanish rule as well as British, Confederate and American custody.

"Hey, do you have any plans tomorrow night," Coletti said, surprising him.

"Not unless watching reruns of 'Big Bang Theory' counts," he said. "And I'm pretty sure I've seen them all at this point."

"How would you like to be my date to a black-tie event?"

"Um, yes."

"It's a fundraiser for HOST, at the Center of Hope," she said. "There will be a lot of big donors there, probably some celebrities. And of course Carl Stanford will attend."

"Sorry, who's Carl Stanford."

"Oh, duh," Coletti said. "I'm so used to dealing with people associated with HOST I forget that our noble philanthropist isn't that well known outside organization circles. Mr. Stanford is the person who founded HOST 20 years ago."

"I'm surprised I haven't run across him at any city functions," Howell said. He regularly covered city council meetings, attended chamber of commerce networking events and interviewed civic and business leaders for the St. Augustine Citizen. It puzzled him that someone as important as Stanford was to the community had never come up in conversation. "He must keep a very low profile."

"He does, in fact," Coletti said. "Very soft-spoken, reclusive gentlemen – an introvert, really. The group's spokesperson, Jacques Philippe, is the one who talks people into donating to the cause," she added. "Stanford found him in Haiti years ago, preaching to impoverished peasants. He's quite charismatic and debonair in an old-fashioned way – kind of like he belongs in another era."

Howell flinched. He could not help but feel he had been exposed to some cryptic enigma by perceiving correlations between seemingly unrelated events.

* * *

After dropping Karina Coletti off at the HOST Center of Hope, Dwight Howell pulled into a nearby shopping center parking lot and found a coffee shop boasting WiFi. Inside, he ordered a flavored ice tea and found a quiet corner where he could do some Internet research without interruption.

According to the HOST website, the Center of Hope had been built in 1992 with funds donated by a laundry list of affluent movers and shakers including hedge fund managers, CEOs, oil billionaires, venture capitalists and other businesspeople and government officials. The center partnered with St. Johns County to create education programs for those interested in working toward their GED. Other plans catered to those seeking specific trade skills, clerical training and basic job readiness.

The biography section of the website named the HOST board of directors but revealed little about Carl Stanford. Details about other board members were restricted mainly to professional affiliations and community service awards. Jacques Philippe, the HOST spokesperson, had immigrated from Haiti in 1995 to spearhead Stanford's St. Augustine project which had gradually spread to other metropolitan hubs across the Southeast, including a recently-opened branch in Atlanta. Philippe utilized his "remarkable oratory skills" to appeal for donations as well as to harvest the homeless to participate in the HOST plan.

On a whim, Howell compared a recent photograph of Jacques Philippe to a 19th century charcoal etching of Jean-Jacques Philippe. He found the striking resemblance more than a little unsettling.

As he finished his iced tea and prepared to head over to the site of the Luddington estate, a homeless woman fell against the glass window of the coffee shop startling him. Her dirty hands smudged the surface as she stood staring down at him muttering something unintelligible. Her bloodshot eyes swelled with anguish and despondency, her pupils pulsing with inexplicable shadows.

5.

> Now came still evening on, and twilight gray
> Had in her sober livery all things clad ...
> From *Paradise Lost*, John Milton, 1667

A forest of soaring deciduous red oaks flanked the meandering ribbon of asphalt as it tapered off into the undeveloped wilderness behind a modest subdivision south of St. Augustine. Dwight Howell poked around the suburban neighborhood for an hour before spotting the indistinct side road. The long-neglected lane had been almost entirely obscured from view by a canopy of kudzu vines.

After inching along the road for more than a mile, the tall oaks and open understory gradually gave way to a blend of laurel oak, sabal palm, redbay and southern magnolia. The vegetation gradually crept in closer to the jagged lip of pavement as the mixed oak hammock overhead enclosed the narrowing throughway and blotted out the late afternoon sky. Storm clouds began to diminish the glimmering patches of light strewn over the fern-blanketed ground.

No more than 30 minutes separated Dwight Howell from battling the brisk stampede of Friday rush hour traffic. Though all the comforts of modern civilization could be found not much more than a mile away, Howell felt as though he had drifted into a parallel universe or slipped back in time a hundred years: The undeveloped Florida backcountry offered a place of quiet, preternatural immersion and overwhelming tranquility.

A vine-covered wall, partially collapsed, emerged from the wilderness. Old *no trespassing* signs lingered, proclaiming a muted warning to infrequent gatecrashers. A rusty chain link fence encircled all, racing off in either direction and disappearing in the foliage. Howell parked his car and approached the main gate. A granite plaque on the nearby wall confirmed what he had presumed. He had located the Luddington Estate.

Beyond the gate, Howell hiked an old country road as it climbed the manmade bluff Erastus Luddington had commissioned more than a century ago. Spreading pines and thick palmetto scrub bordered the path. The surrounding environment served as home to a variety of song birds, deer, wild turkey, hogs and gopher tortoises. Howell expected the only wildlife he would encounter would be less endearing. A healthy aversion to mosquitoes, ticks and venomous snakes routinely kept him from frequenting the state's wilds.

At the top of the bluff, there, amidst the ancient trees, the Luddington mansion squatted like a colossal monument to a bygone era. A former embodiment of opulence, the deserted manor had endured decades of inattention and erosion, stubbornly resisting ruin. Mystery brooded in the place.

Equipped with nothing more than a flashlight and a camera, Howell ascended the moss-covered steps and had no difficulty gaining access to the long vacant dwelling. Inside, the receding afternoon sunlight shone on filthy walls fouled by gangrenous decay. Endless rainstorms had long ago breached the roof and filtered through the upper floors of the residence, painting vile blots and smudges over the vaulted ceiling. The manse proved a peculiar, rambling jumble of architectural styles with a cavernous central hall flanked by extensive Georgian wings.

The first few rooms Howell visited had been scrupulously emptied of their contents, leaving only the dust of decomposition and the stench of staggered decline. He dutifully recorded the heartrending starkness with his camera.

Carefully, he climbed an elaborate staircase, blackened with nebulous splotches of mildew. The rotted wood strained with each footfall, and Howell nearly retreated when a section of handrail dislodged and crashed to the floor taking several disintegrated balusters with it. The air stinking of putrefaction, his flashlight swept over blemishes that seemed eerily similar to the black pustules and festering lesions a plague victim might exhibit as death approached.

In a room that had once served as a voluminous library, Howell found the first trace of lingering furnishings. In a corner, the remnants of a French Empire mahogany fauteille chair – complete with meticulously carved lion heads upon the arms and carved paw feet – had been so ravaged by the passage of time it seemed likely to fall to pieces if so much as a ghost should disturb it. The room also contained a lowboy of old mahogany, a plain wooden settee and an antique steamer trunk.

Standing in the doorway, Howell realized that one entire wall of the room once showcased an elaborate mural. Time had pillaged its vibrant colors and rampant mold had disfigured the ornate frieze so significantly that he could only speculate what it originally depicted. He recognized a full and spectral moon looming above a shadow-haunted forest, its pallid luminescence challenged by a constellation of strangely radiant orbs, each containing a nucleus teeming with ominous, swirling black clouds. Elsewhere, the painting illustrated figures clad in ceremonial robes consorting with unearthly entities.

Howell felt as if he had been granted a reprieve, as if the damage that obscured the mural and kept him from perceiving its depraved majesty had simultaneously shielded him from insanity. He felt a sudden urge to withdraw – to walk away from the mansion and try earnestly to banish its memory from his mind.

As a journalist, he could not deny his reckless curiosity.

He opened the steamer trunk and found a treasure trove of relics in its shadowy depths. The first item he plucked from the darkness was a framed photograph similar to the one Matthew Butler had shown him the day before of the secretive Fraternitas Argenteus Crepusculum group. Luddington stood in the center of the front row.

Howell flipped through the pages of a tattered old pamphlet titled *Look to the Future*. Its pages overflowed with esoteric writings, magical symbols and encrypted passages. As he scanned the text looking for familiar names, the estate's endemic darkness seemed to extend its tenacious sovereignty. He realized dusk would soon envelope the property and invincible, ageless shadows would retaliate against his incursion.

Hurriedly, Howell collected enigmatic documents, tomes and odd fetishes from the trunk, filling his backpack.

He fled back down the staircase into the central hall, alarmed by the quickly vanishing beams of meager sunlight piercing the windows. The last light of the day engendered long, menacing silhouettes along the gloomy corridors. In the unexplored chambers of that sprawling mansion, nightfall had stirred unseen things from slumber. As Howell retraced his steps toward the front door, he tried to convince himself that the growing clatter could be attributed to all kinds of nocturnal tenants: rats, possums, raccoons and bats likely occupied the abandoned manse.

An unearthly screech brought Howell to an abrupt standstill as a wave of paralysis overtook him.

The sound emanated from a nearby hall. To his ears, it seemed an impossible fusion of bestial howl, shrieking gale and human whimpering. It conjured up images of gruesome monstrosities, suffering and madness.

Howell approached the hallway, frightened but mesmerized. He pushed aside a tattered old curtain that concealed a narrow passage of shallow marble steps descending into utter darkness. The screech rang out a second time and was immediately join by a chorus of similarly awful wails.

Howell's inquisitiveness reached its cutoff point at that moment. He flew through the mansion and out the front door and down the old country road past the laurel oak, sabal palm, redbay and southern magnolia. By now, Twilight had overspread the forest. A spectral moon, hauntingly familiar, loomed overhead, providing sufficient light to guide him back down the path to his car.

6.

> Silence was pleased: now glowed the firmament
> With living saphirs: Hesperus, that led
> The starry host, rode brightest, till the moon
> Rising in clouded majesty, at length
> Apparent queen unveiled her peerless light,
> And over the dark her silver mantle threw.
> From *Paradise Lost*, John Milton, 1667

Dwight Howell receded into comforting folds of shadow neatly pinned down by the warm glow of fluorescent lights in the sordid St. Augustine tavern known as Ribault's Revenge. The Friday night crowd proved more rowdy than usual, but he kept his distance, selecting a booth in the spacious dining annex that usually only attracted drunken lovers looking for an out-of-the-way niche.

Sensing his angst, Silas Merry, the bar's owner, had placated him with a bottle of rum and a novelty shot glass. Howell had downed four shots by the time Matthew Butler negotiated the raucous crowd and sat down across from him.

"You look as bad as I feel," Butler said. "But I'm glad you called. There are some things we need to talk about. Things I should have told you yesterday."

"I have some things to show you," Howell said, taking no notice of the assistant professor's hesitant confession. "I paid a visit to the Luddington place earlier this evening."

"You what?" Butler, wan-eyed and hollow-cheeked, cringed at the revelation. "How did you find it?

"I told you, I do know how to do some research, professor." Howell began retrieving the items he had appropriated from the mansion, stacking them on the table. Once he had emptied his backpack, he poured rum into the shot glass and pushed it toward Butler. "Might want to indulge before we begin," Howell said. "It dulls the horror a little."

The journalist began detailing the worm-eaten documents and letters he had collected, starting with a 19th century critical edition of Jean Bodin's "Demonomania of Witches," a Renaissance treatise on the prosecution of witches by an eminent French academic. Within its dog-eared and age-yellowed pages, a section illuminating the scourge of secret societies, Eastern mystic cults and various subversive movements mentioned the group Knights of the Silver Twilight.

A letter – signed enigmatically by C.S. and dated November 1872 – addressed Erastus Luddington as an Elder of the Order and contained instructions on the character and rituals of his "fledgling chapter." The text divided the order into seven degrees including three conventional ones – Neophyte, Initiate or Pupil of the Silver Flame and Master or Philosophus – as well as four higher degrees not known publicly nor to most members. These included Adeptus Major or Keeper of the Silver Gate, Adeptus Exemptus or Knight of the Outer Void, Magus or Son of Yog-Sothoth; and Elder or Wizard.

Look to the Future, the tattered and torn pamphlet, presented esoteric essays hinting at secret histories and ancient cults. Within its prose lived outlandish references to forgotten gods and outré dimensions and appellations unknown yet evocatively familiar: the Throne of Azathoth, the Sunken Abode of Great Cthulhu, the Ark of Vlactos and the Black Tower of Leng.

Various newspaper clippings offered clues about the Luddington family. Howell singled out the 1877 obituary for Erastus Luddington. It concluded with a line stating Luddington would be "missed by his brethren at the Hermetic Order of the Silver Twilight."

Another newspaper article – this one dated 1898 – described a nighttime raid on the Luddington estate, at the time owned by Charles, the eldest child of Erastus and Mary Dolores. An armed militia besieged the mansion following reports of strange rituals taking place on the banks of the Matanzas River. The citizens threatened to burn down the manor unless Charles and his siblings surrendered. According to the story, Charles capitulated on the condition his brothers and sisters be left in peace until proper authorities could investigate.

"Look, Dwight," Butler said, closing his eyes as he took a shot. "You're getting yourself into something you should avoid. Just back off. You've got money. Drop this, get out of town – hell, get out of the state. Go somewhere else and make a fresh start. You have that ability."

"I have a responsibility," Howell said. "To find out how all these pieces fit together. To find out why someone would dig up a 130-year-old grave. To find out why the city covered up a grave robbery that happened 20 years ago. To find out why there are homeless people wandering the streets looking like zombies." He paused, surprised he had uttered the last statement aloud. He rubbed his brow, trying to soothe the dull ache mushrooming deep inside his skull. "I have a responsibility," he repeated.

"No you don't, Dwight," Butler said. "It's my fault, I shouldn't have told you anything. I should have followed my instincts." Butler paused, his eyes sweeping the crowd. "*They* made me tell you. *They* made me give you all that information," he said. "You're being manipulated. You don't need to be the rat in their maze, Dwight. You have no reason to continue."

"Yes, I do," Howell said, but his conviction did not have its foundation in simple obstinacy. Something deeper drove his passion. He picked up the photograph he had found at the mansion, now missing its frame. "Recognize this?"

"Yes, like the one I showed you yesterday. Fraternitas Argenteus Crepusculum."

"Precisely," Howell said. He flipped it over. On the back, someone had – in ornate script – inscribed the names of the people pictured. "Erastus Luddington is standing at the center of the front row," Howell said. "Read the names of the people on his left and right."

"Carl Stanford," Butler said, the name initiating a tremor in his voice. "And ... Daniel Dwight Howell."

Butler lacked the courage to ask his former student to confirm the familial connection. He had no need: He found the answer in Howell's tormented expression.

"I'm going to ask you again, professor: Why did someone desecrate Erastus Luddington's grave?" Howell flipped the photograph over so the brooding faces of Fraternitas Argenteus Crepusculum could burn themselves into Butler's memory. "What were they looking for?"

"Answering that question honestly endangers the both of us," Butler warned. "And I know only a fragment of the truth, thankfully." Butler shrank into his seat, his apprehension escalating with each utterance. "What if I told you a knowledgeable person could, just prior to his death, imprint himself upon an object?"

"Transplant his soul?"

"You can call it a 'soul' if you wish, but we – " Butler winced, realizing his slip of the tongue. "The members of such esoteric organizations prefer to think of it as one's psyche – the sum total of one's wisdom, insight and experience."

"You make it sound as easy as uploading files to a USB flash drive." Howell said. "And once retrieved, I suppose the soul can be resurrected, theoretically. But the body – "

"The original body would be unusable," Butler said. "A new vessel would have to be acquired. Preferably one that is receptive to the transfer. The old 'soul,' as you call it, displaces the existing one."

"What kind of person would agree to that?"

"Someone with no reason to live," Butler said somberly. "Someone mired in wretchedness, suffering and loneliness."

"The outcasts of the world," Howell said. "Those who are as a shadow, and without hope."

7.

> Across the dusky hills
> The first flush of waking
> Unfurls its silver banner
> To signal the Isle for her:
> She vanishes, as before, into the fading Night.
> From *Sandhya: Songs of Twilight*, Dhan Gopal Mukerji

As Dwight Howell and Karina Coletti pulled into the parking lot of the HOST Center of Hope on Dixie Highway south of St. Augustine, he turned to her and summoned up an inconsequential smile.

"Whatever happens this evening, I wanted to thank you for what you did." Fearful his story would cause her undue panic, Howell had prudently kept it all to himself. "I wish I had opened my eyes earlier, but I'm glad you opened them for me when you did."

"You sound so serious," Coletti said, fixing her makeup in the rearview mirror. "Come on, let's enjoy the evening. We have plenty of time to get things back on track."

Howell had spent most of the day Saturday studying his notes and going over the material he had taken from the Luddington mansion. None of it wholly substantiated Matthew Butler's far-fetched conjecture nor validated the wild theories he had concocted. Revealing anything to Coletti would undoubtedly snuff out whatever chance they might have had at reigniting their relationship; moreover, if the story turned out to be true, telling her might endanger her.

Whatever secrets and schemes the inner circle at HOST shielded, Howell felt certain Coletti had no knowledge of it.

"I guess it's time," he said, admittedly tense. Howell never felt comfortable in a classic tuxedo with bow tie and cummerbund. "Shall we?"

Coletti and Howell strode the building's main entrance, clearing a security check-point and following festive signs toward the evening's gala event. The seven-story Center of Hope featured an ornate 10,000-square-foot grand ballroom at its heart, complete with paneled walls, parquet wood floors, two chandeliers and a raised stage. A 10-piece swing orchestra had the dance floor jumping with a Count Basie classic.

"We should dance," Coletti said, taking his arm without allowing him to resist.

Howell had little choice, and – for the next few minutes at least – he found his trepidation dislodged by the music, the lightheartedness of the atmosphere and the pleasure of being with the woman he still loved. Coletti had not been spreading propaganda when she claimed big names would appear at the fundraiser. As they circled the dance floor, he spotted several regional celebrities including television news personalities, professional sports figures, well-known businesspeople and city and county office-holders.

The presence of such persons further scattered Howell's conspiratorial suspicions. It seemed less and less likely that HOST could be engaged in such blasphemies as grave robbery and sinister ceremonial magic. Howell found himself enjoying the scene, relishing his renewed relationship with Coletti and meeting new acquaintances which could help further his career as a journalist.

After three hours of cocktails, delectable appetizers and introductions, Howell had almost forgotten about Erastus Luddington and Fraternitas Argenteus Crepusculum.

At 10 p.m., Jacques Philippe stepped behind a podium on the stage and addressed the attendees. The well-groomed, cultured Haitian hardly struck Howell as a bloodthirsty butcher.

"Good evening," Philippe began. "We have quite a turnout this evening. Let me be the first to thank you all for your support. HOST is most appreciative for your continuing contributions and we want you all to know that your generosity has made a difference in our community."

Philippe continued, recounting recent achievements and highlighting fundraising goals for the next six months. He mentioned small satellite offices opening in rural communities elsewhere in Florida and promised more would follow throughout the Southern states.

"Next year, we plan to extend our charitable foundation overseas, opening offices in Estonia, Azerbaijan, Kazakhstan and Mongolia," Philippe said. "This will bring the total number of international offices to 22."

Philippe recognized a handful of substantial donors and welcomed new benefactors before introducing a short graphics presentation. He left the stage, the lights dimmed and a mammoth high-definition digital screen descended. The room filled with weirdly cadenced piping, as though some unseen flautist performed a composition written for an alien audience. Specks of light gradually emerged from the darkness on the screen, forging a starry night sky against the silhouette of a city skyline.

Like an amateur Microsoft PowerPoint presentation, HOST began outlining its principal fundraising points with a series of bulleted statements:

Do you dare to imagine things as they can be?

Poverty is an illusion sustained by institutional ignorance.

A mind freed from the shackles of despair recognizes its ultimate significance.

A mind freed from the shackles of despair can succeed and thrive.

The world can be transformed, one mind at a time.

Look to the future.

The accompanying video images illustrated the HOST model: Take the homeless off of the streets, provide them with food and shelter, test their aptitude and identify their abilities, train them in the appropriate areas and help them reintegrate into society. The system apparently worked. HOST claimed it had helped more than 10,000 individuals in six countries find employment and permanent housing.

After the presentation, Coletti excused herself to visit with coworkers, leaving Howell to fend for himself. Scanning the crowd, he noticed a former classmate at Drayton College. The chance encounter offered him a perk: His old friend worked for a high-circulation newspaper.

By the time Coletti returned, Howell had met half the editorial staff of the Jacksonville Tribune.

"Dwight," Coletti said, pulling him away from his conversation. "Come with me, sweetie."

"Karina, this is – " Howell began, but Coletti was already pulling him away into maze of tables. "Sorry, I'll call you," Howell said, slightly embarrassed.

"Sorry, it's important," Coletti said, her tone unexpectedly stern. "Mr. Stanford wants to meet you," she said. "Mr. Stanford doesn't often ask to be introduced to guests." She led him down a dimly lit hallway, passing a burly security guard who nodded at her with a hint of veneration. As they waited for the elevator, she groomed him tenderly, brushing his hair and adjusting his bow tie. "I can't overemphasize how significant this invitation is," Coletti said. "Stanford is *not* a people person. He avoids company."

"What can you tell me about him," Howell asked, his fears rushing up to the surface. "I mean, what do you know about this guy?"

"Mr. Stanford is very cerebral, very insightful," she said. They stepped into the elevator, and Coletti tapped the button for the seventh floor. "He's a visionary. He finds others to implement his initiatives. He attracts extraordinary people to his inner circle."

"You could be describing the leader of a cult, you realize," Howell said. The elevator doors opened.

"Or a saint," Coletti said. "All a matter of perspective, I suppose."

She escorted him down a corridor embellished with a peculiar collection of bas-relief scenes depicting what Howell believed to be some ancient Assyrian or Sumerian city. One involved a curious cryptozoological hybrid, mingling bits of an octopus, a dragon and a human caricature to form a repugnant abomination with a scaly body and immature wings.

"Mr. Stanford is expecting you Mr. Howell," a receptionist said. "I'm sorry, Ms. Coletti. You'll have to wait here."

"Oh," Coletti said, visibly shaken. "Well, all right." She turned toward Howell and – much to his surprise – kissed him on the cheek. "You can do this."

Howell walked into Stanford's office. The receptionist closed the doors behind him.

"Mr. Stanford, it's an honor – " Howell felt the blow to the back of his head only for an instant, then darkness enveloped him.

* * *

When Dwight Howell awoke, he found himself in what appeared to be a board room, seated at a long table. Much of the room remained shrouded in shadow. On the walls, though, four flat-screen monitors shimmered with aberrant luminosity. Each depicted a scene of decadence and depravity – midnight revelers participating in blasphemous rituals beneath ash-colored stars, misshapen horrors roaming the ruins of emptied cities, mass graves and unburied corpses and burning skies. Beneath the loathsome images, fiendish distortions of HOST's public standards scrolled across the screens:

Do you dare to imagine things as they can be?

Reality is an illusion sustained by institutional ignorance.

A mind freed from the shackles of hope recognizes its ultimate insignificance.

A mind liberated from the chains of faith is vulnerable and accessible.
The world can be transformed, one mind at a time.
Look to the future.

"I have to apologize, Mr. Howell." Carl Stanford sat at the far end of the table. "I did not intend to employ such uncivilized measures unless circumstances forced my hand. Unfortunately, I failed to effectively communicate my wishes to my associates," he said, nodding his head toward two security officers standing at attention in the corner of the room. Howell shuddered as he discerned their eyes, darkened by impossible shadows. "They serve me devotedly and function competently enough. They just are not capable of understanding the nuances of complex instructions sometimes."

"How old are you?"

"Interesting," Stanford said. "Of all the questions you could ask, that is where you begin." Stanford smiled, but his expression exposed an ominous malevolence that betrayed no hint of amusement. "I suppose it is logical. Were I to give an accurate answer, you could infer your various suppositions could in turn be corroborated. Of course, I cannot give you an accurate answer – in part because I do not actually know for certain how old I am."

"Fine," Howell said. "We can do this the hard way, then. What did you remove from Erastus Luddington's grave? Something that enabled you to resurrect his soul?"

"I am sorry to disappoint you, Mr. Howell," Stanford said. "I understand you are a journalist and, as such, you have an exasperating inquisitiveness. I have not brought you here this evening to answer your questions," Stanford said. "In fact, I have already supplied you with so many pieces of the puzzle you should have worked most of it out for yourself by now. Matthew Butler, in particular, helped to facilitate this meeting by drawing you deeper into the investigation. Butler will be rewarded for his contribution."

"So you've brought me here to dispose of me, then," Howell said. "Just promise me you won't hurt Karina."

"Ms. Coletti?" Stanford sighed. "Though I question her choice of mates, I have no intention in harming my personal assistant, Mr. Howell. Furthermore, I did not bring you here to kill you. I have invested far too much to discard you." Stanford leaned to one side and fished for something on the floor. He tossed Howell's backpack on the table. "I have recovered the materials you were allowed to find at the Luddington estate. I trust you examined them thoroughly."

"I did," Howell said. "I saw the photograph. I saw you, Luddington and my great-grandfather."

"I knew your great-grandfather quite well," Stanford said. "Brilliant man, ahead of his time in his field." Stanford sorted through the material until he located the photograph. "Erastus, too. The two of them perfected an elixir," he said, stopping himself. "Pardon the obsolete term – they perfected a pharmaceutical compound that extends life. Of course, it came with certain disadvantages: negative aspects that kept the two of them from using it themselves."

"They helped you, and you made them leaders in your order, Fraternitas Argenteus Crepusculum," Howell said. "Now, you've found a way to bring back these people, lodge their souls in the bodies of these homeless people you claim to help. How many have already resurrected? How many souls have you displaced to furnish your old friends with – "

"Stop, please," Stanford said, cutting him short. "All good speculation, but if you agree to join us, you will understand everything."

"Join you?"

"Yes, Mr. Howell. That is why you are here. Your family has been involved in the Hermetic Order of the Silver Twilight for more than a century," Stanford said. "The Howell family, along with the Luddingtons, the Scotts, the Emersons and others, have been vital to recalling the Great Old Ones and hastening the restoration of their dominion over this world."

"I don't know what you're talking about, Stanford," Howell said, annoyed that the man had implicated his parents in his sickening cult. Howell's parents had died when he was very young. He assembled fragmentary memories from snapshots in scrapbooks and stories his godparents had shared with him. He had no reason to believe they could have been involved in anything as sordid as Stanford's secret society. "My parents led normal lives, decent lives. They wouldn't have joined your cause."

"Your parents, Mr. Howell, remained loyal to the cause until the time of their deaths," Stanford said, growing aggravated. "They gave their lives in a ceremony that opened a conduit we employ to this day." Stanford stood and wordlessly instructed his guards to secure his guest. "In a few hours, you will see how we truly utilize our homeless martyrs. You will understand, then, I believe," Stanford said. "Then, you will have a choice to make."

* * *

The mute security guards escorted Dwight Howell down a long subterranean corridor. Somewhere in the shadows ahead of them, a group of 13 hooded figures marched single file toward their shared destination. Though Howell had not seen them, he knew the group included Carl Stanford. He guessed Jacques Philippe also joined the procession.

When the opportunity presented itself, Howell gazed into the faces of his loutish wardens. Their eyes contained the shadows of monstrous things. He beheld the distant sanctuary of tenebrous entities long ago exiled into the vast gulfs of nothingness beyond exhausted galaxies littered with suffocated stars, charred worlds and aborted empires. He beheld intolerable things that lurked just outside the collective memory of humanity –ravenous things eager to drive all life and light from the universe. Stanford conjured that nebulosity, ousting their identities and replacing it with some awful alien essence.

As he traversed that clandestine passageway, Howell felt suddenly inconsequential and utterly ignorant.

Days earlier, his greatest concern had been picking up good leads to score story placement on the front page of the St. Augustine Citizen. He had spent countless hours grieving over his broken relationship with Karina Coletti and he had spent years earning a bachelor's degree to give himself a sense of purpose.

Now, he realized how irrelevant it had all been, how unimportant he was as an individual. Expanding upon that staggering logic, Howell viewed humanity as equally negligible – a marginally evolved species on a remote world communally incapable of momentous advancement.

Surprisingly, Howell's unsettling epiphany separated him from his fear. His acceptance of this shared human condition actually made him more empathetic and inspired him to fight for survival.

A growing chorus of repugnant shrieks confirmed what Dwight Howell had already surmised: The passageway connected the HOST Center of Hope to the chamber beneath the old Luddington mansion. Inside the cavernous, man-made chamber, he could see that the howls emanated from rows of pits in the floor. What monstrosities had been deposited in those dank cavities he preferred not to know.

Carl Stanford ascended a set of stone steps to a marble altar, calling his disciples to gather around him. Two figures – nearly identical to the guards handling Howell – emerged from the shadows ushering in dazed supplicants – hand-picked drifters who had sought shelter at HOST.

"Tonight, we gather to call down in iridescent globes the protoplasmic essence of Yog-Sothoth," Carl Stanford said, and his followers began a well-rehearsed chant. "We offer these vessels to hasten his return."

Howell recoiled as a vortex appeared behind the altar and spawned a cloud of queerly radiant orbs, each containing a nucleus crawling with ethereal, churning murk. The orbs quickly descended, engulfing the victims. The transformation took only a few seconds. The results were immediately evident, even at a distance. Howell saw how the shadows of Yog-Sothoth had infested their eyes.

"The world can be transformed, one mind at a time," Stanford proclaimed exultantly.

"Look to the future," his disciples chanted in unison. The beasts in the pits howled in consensus.

"Tonight, we gather to welcome at least one new member to the higher degrees of our order," Stanford said. He beckoned to a hooded figure who had lingered in the background during the first part of the ceremony. "Kneel, Master of the Silver Flame," Stanford said. The petitioner followed his command. Stanford presented the disciple with a ceremonial key. "Arise, Keeper of the Silver Gate."

As the figure stood, Stanford pulled back the hood.

Karina Coletti bowed in reverence.

The other disciples then removed their hoods, revealing their identities. Among them was Jacques Philippe, a former St. Augustine city councilman, a Jacksonville-based businesswoman and Joel Nye, the managing editor of the St. Augustine Citizen.

Also present was a man Howell had seen a few nights earlier. The emaciated vagrant wearing ragged, loose-fitting clothes outside the Tolomato Cemetery stood confidently beside his peers, his eyes remarkably similar in hue and intensity to those of Erastus Luddington.

Stanford whispered one further command to Coletti, pointing in Howell's direction. In a moment she stood before him, her hand outstretched, urging him to follow. Howell felt trapped: He had been manipulated from the beginning, compelled to follow the clues, persuaded to speculate on unimaginable horrors and finally asked to participate in and contribute to the wicked enterprises of Stanford and his Hermetic Order of the Silver Twilight.

"It's truly a noble cause, Dwight," Coletti said, tugging on his arm. "And it's in your blood. You belong here, as part of this crusade to set things right."

"I can't believe the woman I knew a year ago would condone this," Howell said, his voice a whisper. "I can't believe you would devote your life to that madman, to help him transform these transients into hosts for some pantheon of embittered gods."

"Don't you see," Coletti said, stroking his cheek with the back of her hand. "We're the abomination, Dwight. We're polluting this world. We are minor, petty beings so far removed from perfection that we cannot recognize the purity of the Great Old Ones. We're liberating these wretched people from false hope. They are our martyrs, sacrificing themselves to help us recall Yog-Sothoth one cell at a time."

"What about those things down there in those cells?" Howell inched closer to one of the nearby pits, glancing over the edge. He cringed at the misshapen creature he saw in the darkness. "Are they martyrs, too? Or are they botched transfers, imperfect vessels driven insane by the horrors contaminating them?"

"The transformation isn't always successful," she explained. "Sometimes, they change their minds at the last moment. The disruption causes physical deformities, mutations, blindness, madness."

"Stanford," Howell yelled. He grasped Coletti by the shoulders, pushed her to the edge of the pit. "I will not be a part of this. Take your disciples and leave the chamber or I'll kill her. Once you're gone, I'll leave here. She can choose whether she wants to return to you or stay with me."

"Your rejection is unfortunate, but anticipated," Stanford said. "You know what to do Ms. Coletti."

With the fanatical zeal of a cultist, Coletti brushed his hands aside, gripping him viciously above his right elbow in one fluid movement. Her other hand grasped the back of his head as she spun him around toward the rim of the precipice.

"I'm sorry, Dwight," she said, sending him over the ledge and into the darkness. "You're either with us or against us."

The horror it housed howled with sick, twisted pleasure at it began tearing at its unexpected meal.

* * *

After an eternity of darkness, Dwight Howell awoke to a chorus of hideous howls and shrieks. His bones broken, his limbs torn asunder, his flesh half-devoured, he found life somehow still lingered. His companion – the misshapen horror that had once been shunned as a pariah – had apparently filled its belly.

"Dwight?" Karina Coletti's voice echoed through the chamber. He turned his gaze upward and saw her eyes peering over the ledge. "I've been waiting for you. I thought you might reconsider."

"Why," Howell said, choking on blood. Pain somehow deadened his senses. "Why am I still alive?"

"Mr. Stanford injected you with the Essence of Irem," she said. "It will keep you alive for some time, even in that condition. Mr. Stanford will gladly pardon you if you agree to join," she said. "He can fix everything. He can restore you."

"Karina," Dwight muttered, wondering if he every really knew the woman he had loved. "Karina – leave me. Let me wait for death in peace."

ST. AUGUSTINE – Four years after his disappearance, the remains of St. Augustine Citizen reporter Dwight Howell were recovered Wednesday on land bordering the Matanzas State Forest.

Authorities stated that they are treating the case as a homicide.

Howell disappeared shortly after graduating from Drayton College. He was last seen attending a fundraising event at the HOST Center of Hope. Howell's acquaintance, Karina Coletti, told authorities at the time he had left the event around 11 p.m. intending to go home.

St. Johns County Sheriff's Department spokesperson Sgt. Andy Wilson stated that the crime is still under investigation. Anyone with information concerning the homicide is asked to contact the sheriff's office.

The Damascus Code

1.

"Carver: If you're there, pick up."

The phone call stirred me from fitful slumber plagued by pedestrian nightmares concerning missed mortgage payments and the recent ruin of yet another marriage. The combination of exhaustion and the aftereffects of countless whisky shots clouded my lucidity and slowed my reaction. Fumbling in the darkness, half a dozen items perched along the edge of the nightstand tumbled to the floor before I managed to locate the phone.

"Yeah, hello." Beneath the bedroom door, light from the television flickered in the hallway. Leaving the thing on all night had become a pathetic habit, a compulsive attempt to dupe myself into believing I was not alone. The self-deception clearly suggested some embryonic neurosis that would eventually require therapy. "Hello? Is anyone there?"

"Preston – is that you?"

"Yes. Who's calling?"

"Preston, it's good to hear your voice. This is Bernie." There was a pause as I rifled through my memory trying to attach a face to the name. "Wesley Bernard Weaver, from school."

"Bernard?" A classmate from my days at Tusgagunee University in Georgia, I had not spoken to or thought about Weaver in two decades. Unlike him, I stayed on at Tusgagunee to earn my master's. After finally completing his prolonged undergraduate studies with a less than stellar performance, Bernard's father penned a dozen endowment checks until some New England institution lowered its standards enough to let him glide through the admissions process. "How did you get my number?"

"The Internet is omniscient. A few more keystrokes and I could probably locate your cholesterol levels from your last physical." The clock on the dresser read 3:22

a.m. In about two hours, I would be wrenched from slumber by the irksome screech of its merciless alarm. Following a lukewarm shower courtesy of an undersized water heater, I would drive two miles in heavy traffic to the local high school where teenagers would ignore me through most of seven periods of literature classes. Though the prospect of catching up with Bernard appealed to me on some level, the thought that he might rob me of one more moment of sleep invoked an immediate animosity. "I know it's late," he said, interrupting me as I began to doze off again. "It's just that – well, you're the only person I can think of that might be able to help. The only one I can trust, anyway."

"What is this about, Bernard?"

"Something I've been working on. Something extraordinary."

"Where are you?"

"Near Cohutta, not far from Asheville. That's another reason I called. Since you're in Greeneville, you're only a few hours away."

"Bernard, I haven't seen you in 20 years..."

"I know, I know." An unexpected angst crept into his voice, a faceless fear that translated into exasperated stutters and long pauses. "Look, Preston ... I wouldn't call unless I thought that you would, um, benefit ... not financially, but academically, as a scholar. This is something that should be of considerable interest to you, considering your ... background. I know you focused on Shakespeare in school, but your true passion was classic esoteric literature ... that's why I need your input. I wish I could explain it more thoroughly, but I'm not comfortable going into it on the phone. That sounds paranoid, but ... you just have to trust me." His line of reasoning disintegrated into a hesitant plea. "If anything I've said has interested you, drive up this weekend. I'm working in a private facility near the town. I'll e-mail you the directions."

"I'll see what I can do," I said. Still half-asleep, I could think of nothing else to say.

"Nice talking to you. Sorry if I bothered you."

The conversation ended, but Bernard had managed to annihilate any hope of returning to sleep by wheedling into my brain with unfathomable intimations and bizarre ravings. His entreaty had not been as unsettling as the tone in which he delivered it. Something wild and frenzied in his voice left me questioning his sanity as well as the urgency of his request.

Though the precise nature of his "extraordinary" work remained a mystery, I imagined the overly eager, often obsessive Bernard squandering away hours in some laboratory evoking the very gods of physics and mathematics to derive some incredible, yet wholly impractical, creation. His grades may have been lackluster, but his genius – buried beneath social inadequacies and a trace of misanthropy – could never be doubted by his peers or the professors who derided him as lethargic and disrespectful. His zealous absorption of fringe theories and pseudoscience earned him little more than ridicule at Tusgagunee.

How my admiration of medieval occult literature might somehow support his scientific endeavor I could not guess. As I dressed for work, I convinced myself that I should gracefully decline the invitation, avoiding what I envisioned as an awkward reunion at best.

By the last class of the day I felt my resolve fading. My students fidgeted in uncomfortable desks, pens racing across notebook pages as I delivered a standard lecture on Hawthorne's *The Scarlet Letter*. Perhaps half bothered to read the assigned work. One or two had outright refused, with parental support, claiming the novel touted a morally bankrupt character. Their snub, of course, encouraged twice as many to read it.

In the midst of my classroom sermon, I discarded my index cards and eased into the chair at my desk.

"Anyone read anything else by Hawthorne?"

Heads bobbed, papers shuffled, notebooks unfolded like a brigade of butterflies preparing to migrate.

"Did you assign it?" Geoff Heinz sat near the front of the class in the row closest to the obsolete blackboard.

"No, I meant in another class." I studied their vacant stares, befuddled gazes and anxious fingers pawing at the official course syllabus. "I thought you might have been exposed to Hawthorne's shorter works. Like 'The Minister's Black Veil'?"

"I read 'Tall Tale Heart' last year in Ms. Allen's class," John Schmautz said. He immediately regretted the admission, fearing I might ask him to give details.

"That's 'The Tell-Tale Heart.' But that wasn't Hawthorne. That was Edgar Allan Poe." I glanced at the clock. Mere minutes separated me from the weekend and from a decision that suddenly seemed more portentous than I had realized. Well into my 40s, a refugee from two aborted attempts at marital bliss, I wondered if the rest of my years might be spent summarizing the works of famous American writers before inattentive and indifferent pupils, abridging literary masterpieces and reducing their significance into short and easily digested blurbs that students readily regurgitated during exams. "Here's an unscheduled assignment for the weekend, for extra credit let's say. Find and read Hawthorne's story 'The Birthmark.'" I could not banish from my mind the caricature of Aylmer, Hawthorne's prototypical mad scientist. I wondered if Bernard had degenerated into something analogous. "We'll discuss it Monday."

2.

"What do you know about instrumental transcommunication?" Bernard escorted me along a sidewalk skirting the perimeter of the privately funded facility located in a relatively isolated expanse in the highlands of western North Carolina. Beyond a tall, electrified fence crowned with a strip of barbed wire, the mountainous terrain of Pisgah National Forest surrounded the heavily fortified compound. On my arrival, I had been quizzed by two security guards manning the front gate. Others, I expected, monitored the property through closed circuit cameras mounted along the building's rooftop.

"You know," he said, "electronic voice phenomenon and things of that nature."

I had expected to find a solitary, reclusive and fixated scientist with a pale countenance and an emaciated form; with unkempt gray hair that reached below his shoulders and a maniacal glint in his eyes that attested to his unconditional commitment to cloistered scientific study. Instead I found my old classmate impeccably well groomed, clean-shaven and dressed in professional attire. He spoke with a confidence and conviction that belied his apprehensive tenor during the previous late-night telephone conversation.

"You mean recordings of ghost voices?"

"Well, that's what some people consider them. There may well be other sources for such occurrences – I know there to be other sources, in fact." Bernard looked furtively over his shoulder. He guided me toward a picnic bench overlooking a creek bed running parallel to the fence. "Several years ago I developed a new technology for the military, a kind of encryption device that utilized experimental high frequency pulses to transmit orders directly to troops in the field. The transmissions were inaudible to the average person – only select soldiers could receive and decipher the messages. To them, it is as if someone was standing next to them, giving the orders. I created both the transmitter and the nanotechnology that gave the soldiers the ability to hear a wider range of frequencies."

"That's amazing." Considering his uninspiring performance at Tusgagunee, that Bernard had managed to develop such a viable innovation enhanced his legitimacy and minimized my skepticism. "Must have made you a few bucks, too."

"Actually the military seized the whole program, confiscated and classified our documentation and forcibly evicted my researchers from their own labs. They allegedly discontinued the experiments, but I've been told that a modified version has been used in Iraq and Afghanistan." Bernard shook his head, silently cursing the bureaucracy that first encouraged, then stifled his initiative.

"Fortunately, I persuaded an organization in the private sector to fund more research. I had backup data and we were able to pick up where we left off."

"I'm still not sure how all of this involves me." Overhead, the silvery skies began to darken. Autumn winds raced through the balsams, howling over distant ridgelines, swirling through sloping valleys and scouring darkened hollows. On grim October days in the Appalachians, winds could transmute into wicked whispers, hinting at the prospect of winter. I leaned against the end of the table, folded my arms over my chest and unsuccessfully tried to suffocate a shiver. "Judging by the amount of security around here, I don't think your employers are too keen on giving tours, either."

"We had some aberrations early on, things we didn't share with the Congressional oversight committee that eventually shut us down. They wouldn't have understood."

"What kind of aberrations?"

"Our test subjects began hearing messages that we weren't sending – messages from an unknown source. Mostly they heard single words or monosyllabic grunts; a few heard sustained mutterings, mostly gibberish. Except for one." Bernard shuddered as another cold breeze swept over across the landscape. "One of our subjects – a second generation New Yorker whose grandparents emigrated from the Middle East – reported hearing voices speaking in Syriac. Are you familiar with that language?"

"If I remember, it's an Eastern Aramaic language. Not common these days, although it's still spoken in a few communities in Syria and Iraq."

"I asked the subject to record what he heard," Bernard continued without confirming my definition. His mind drifted as if he had difficulty picturing the man , remembering his name or recalling what became of him. Still, Bernard had no problem recounting the words the test subject conveyed. "He reported hearing the phrase 'the banished ones are shadows inside the houses of men.' Does that sound familiar to you at all?"

"Well," I hesitated, detecting the connection Bernard hoped I would make. In his e-mail detailing directions to the facility, he had added a peculiar request. I had to search through a dozen boxes before I located my copy of Nicolas l'Agneau's *Conversations avec les Morts*. The statement echoed one of the most often quoted couplets from the work. "I can see the similarity to l'Agneau, if that's what you're getting at."

"How does it go? 'Those whose empire was torn apart, linger on as shadows in our hearts.'"

"That sounds right," I said, feigning forgetfulness. l'Agneau's dark work had originally been shunned by Parisians for its decadent content. Collected in 333 stanzas, its narrative followed the author's grisly experimentations with necromancy. "It's been a long time since I read l'Agneau. It's not the kind of material you can really share with high school seniors. Still, *Conversations* was written in France in 1664. There's no reason to think it was ever translated into Aramaic."

"It wasn't," Bernard said, a mordant smile blossoming. His gaze fell to the earth, his eyes tainted with misgivings like a man revolted by his own thoughts. "I underwent the procedure years ago, extended my own range of hearing so that I might verify the phenomenon. I taught myself Syriac to better understand." He looked at me with the wretchedness of a caged animal subjected to the follies of biotechnology. "The voice is relentless, the ghost of a whisper, speaking in various archaic tongues – like a recording playing over and over again."

"You hear it now?"

"I hear it always." Bernard massaged his forehead, wrestling with the torturous babble ricocheting around inside his skull. "I know all of this is difficult to believe. It's time I showed you something."

I followed as Bernard led me through three checkpoints inside the facility, each time punching in a code on a numbered keypad, each time verbally confirming his identity, each time nodding to an unseen sentry scrutinizing my presence. Passing through each layer of security, my angst burgeoned. What secrets had to be sheltered so systematically, what hidden horrors had Bernard's imagination exhumed? Now, his own uneasiness became more noticeable. His nervous, shaking fingers hovered over the last control panel and he peered through a small glass window.

"Inside, you're going to see a series of 27 scrolls, some intact, some partially disintegrated and reconstructed from fragments." Bernard gripped my shoulder, impatient but perceptibly cautious. Having been robbed of his first remarkable invention, I understood his vigilance. "It took us months to find it, hunting through archives in Damascus, Baghdad, Cairo and London. No one else knows of its existence; no one else even knows to look for it."

Contained in individual cases shielded by thick glass, 27 ancient pieces of parchment ringed the sterilized vault. Their restoration must have demanded countless hours of dedication and a degree of concentration and care that went beyond mere occupational merit. I examined each time-worn document with infinite admiration and awe. Though I had no background in reading the old Syriac text, the age and allure of the scrolls attracted me no less.

"This, we now believe, is the source material l'Agneau exploited to compose *Conversations avec les Morts*. I pulled strings, paid off some disreputable antiquities dealers across the Middle East and finally confirmed the existence of a document that matched the description." He reflected as he watched me explore each fragile page, trace each delicately penned inscription. He gestured toward a particular section. "The tract the voice repeats is on this page."

"Has it been dated?"

"Unfortunately, tests have been inconclusive, with chemical analyses of the ink dating back to the eighth century, and radiocarbon dating of parchment pieces showing results ranging from 13 centuries to almost 10,000 years." Bernard pointed out visible differences in the parchment, though the penmanship seemed consistent throughout the work. "Our research suggests it was written in Damascus around 730 C.E. by an anonymous Syriac Christian mystic – a contemporary of al-Azrad, in fact."

Like cyclic cyclones pummeling remote islands in the South Pacific, the twists and tangles of fate lined up before my eyes and tested my deep-seated skepticism. I had no doubt Bernard had meticulously evaluated each puzzle piece, methodically investigating each correspondence, corroborating each link in the chain he had constructed. Still, his obsessive nature might have caused him to make faulty observations. Standing there, captivated by both his unspoken conjecture and the repercussions of his tale, I had to admit to myself that the connection seemed tenuous at best – a curious coincidence linking a handful of fragmentary lines in documents set down hundreds of years and miles apart.

"How can you be certain?"

"Until now, I could not completely verify the correlation between this document and the work of l'Agneau."

"So you brought me here for my copy of *Conversations avec les Morts*." An undeniable rarity, the book had been republished occasionally over the years by obscure presses – though the reissues usually contained errors and omissions. Mine was an original copy, handed down from my great grandfather who collected such antiquarian tomes. "Why me? There are other copies available."

"Half a dozen intact copies remain in North America. I couldn't risk contacting William Whitley College or Miskatonic, for that matter. Inquiries would be made. Academics would gossip – they always do. I won't tolerate prying eyes." The glint of fanaticism I had expected to see in his eyes suddenly materialized. In that instant, I knew he had withheld some crucial piece of information – something that might deter me from helping him achieve his objective. "You must understand: There is more to it than simple confirmation. These scrolls were found in disarray, lacking proper order. I believe that by comparing the two texts, we can properly sequence the original."

"And then?"

"Let's take this one step at a time, Preston."

"Listen, if you want my help, you'll have to level with me. What are you planning to do once I've put all this in order?"

"Read it in its entirety. I'll use my transmitter to broadcast these words to that other world, that distant dimension that has been waiting to hear some sign of sentience. That's what they're waiting for." Bernard believed there to be a passage of considerable importance encoded within the text, one that if transmitted might necessitate a transcommunicative response from some supernatural source. To underscore his commitment, Bernard sat down at a small desk on the far side of the room, fingers racing over the keyboard. An instant later, I heard a confident and commanding voice muttering what sounded like nonsense – its intonations visible in a digitized graph displayed upon a monitor screen. "I made this recording years ago, before the government took over the project. The test subject – U.S. Army communications specialist Anthony Khan – replicated the words he heard in his head, recorded them in Aramaic. He said it repeats itself in loops, like a distress signal – like the very signals we beam into outer space in our search for alien life. I set out to develop a new form of communication, and I seem to have found an invisible shimmer in dark and weary world, a connection to the distant past."

I cringed at the sound of the recording, recoiled like prey facing a traditional predator.

"Some things are better left undiscovered." My feeble assertion fell on deaf ears as Bernard immersed himself in the antiquated dialect, listening absorbedly, as if entranced. I knew ultimately I would comply out of incurable curiosity. I knew, too, that Bernard would furnish me with the tools I required to complete the task. "I'll do my best, but I have my reservations. We're doing this for different reasons."

"Even a skeptic can become a believer, Preston. Wait and see."

3.

I awoke to the sound of my own muted screams.

Bernard had provided me with a stipend, allowing me to take a much-earned leave of absence from my teaching career. I had rented a small efficiency in the little mountain town of Cohutta, a modest flat with a gas stove, a Murphy bed and an alley view. The elderly landlord maintained the property well, making it appealing to seasonal tourists by embellishing it with country crafts and various Appalachian accoutrements.

Neither the rustic décor nor the landlord's periodic offers of "a nice cup of tea chased with a snifter of brandy" could displace the persistent nightmares that had plagued me since my arrival. Nightly visions of abandoned cities haunted me, images of emptied streets and silenced screams and the dreadful stillness of a desolate world decimated by some unnamed tragedy. Through these unsettling dreams resonated a mellifluous mantra, subtly spoken yet unrelenting – unfamiliar words uttered in an alien tongue that seemed to conjure chaos and set shadows squirming.

The dreams, I believed, merely mirrored events unfolding daily, illustrated so vibrantly and narrated with such voyeuristic delight on cable news networks. Clawing at the edges of civilization were natural disasters, emerging epidemics, terrorist threats and bloody wars motivated by religion, greed and ideological differences. Anarchy, like an undiagnosed tumor, lurked in the bleak newsprint beneath banner headlines.

Still, an ominous but formless menace haunted my consciousness prompting fits of despondency and dread that made nights crawl.

With hours separating me from dawn and the distraction of my ongoing vocation, I slipped on a pair of jeans and a T-shirt and wandered downstairs and out onto the front steps of the aging apartment building. To my surprise, I found the landlord stationed in a lawn chair in the middle of the parking lot.

"Couldn't sleep? Me neither," he said. The old man noticed the pack of cigarettes in my hand and offered me a light. "Gets harder as you get older. Have to tinkle every half hour, for Christ's sake. Bed's not giving you trouble, is it?"

"The apartment's fine," I said, wishing I had grabbed a sweater. "Just can't sleep."

"Yeah, well, you're not the only one," he said, gesturing back toward the complex. I followed his gaze and counted the number of curtained windows flickering with glow of televisions. Insomnia seemed endemic in the building. "Been like that for a while now. Ever since that young man did himself in."

"Sorry?"

"Oh, you weren't here then. Happened a few months before you moved in." The landlord's face twitched unnaturally and his eyes closed for a moment. A trembling hand scratched at his wrinkled brow. "Arab fellow – quiet, kept his place clean and neat. Lots of books. Police came looking for him one morning and found him dead. Said he'd shot himself in the head."

"You don't happen to remember his name, do you?"

"Sure. Fahid Al-Salhi. Worked up at that old observatory." The old man let his eyes trace the omnipresent stars, searching for familiar arrangements. Spread like diminutive diamonds across the vast black abyss, they shone with a collective condescending radiance that suddenly made the earth seem overwhelmingly insignificant. "Poor man had awful headaches. He was always pounding on my door in the middle of the night begging for aspirin." Even as he uttered the words, I felt a nagging twinge inside my skull – a dull, throbbing ache that had been easy to ignore up to that point. "You work at that place, don't you? Surprised they didn't tell you about it."

I thanked the landlord for his late-night hospitality and returned to my room. As I drifted along the treacherous chasm of sleep, I wondered how many other translators Bernard had lured before he remembered my name. The following day, I said nothing about the revelation. I had already come too far to extract myself from my dark destiny.

4.

While I spent long days engaged in unraveling the mystery of the parallel texts, working collaboratively with a soft-spoken scholar from Lebanon whose understanding of the archaic dialect enabled me to establish key correspondences, Bernard worked tiresomely with his development team constantly trying to improve his innovation. By manipulating newly developed recording devices, he explained, he had discovered additional vocalizations. Though the recent electronic voice phenomena clearly indicated an attempt at communication, the languages spoken could not be identified.

"Here's a dozen different voices speaking in as many different dialects," Bernard said holding a digitized recording captured the previous night. "It's almost as if they know they have an audience now. They're trying different languages, hoping for a response."

"Even if you're right, even if somehow something beyond our perception is trying to make a connection with us – why now? Why haven't they found some other medium more accessible to us?" I sipped cola from a Styrofoam cup hoping the caffeine would alleviate a raging headache. Lack of restful sleep had begun taking a toll on me, though I refrained from discussing my nightmares. Bernard could see my fatigue and I saw it reflected in his face. He rarely left the facility, took short naps on a cot in a cramped room he shared with a row of filing cabinets overflowing with copies of pages from various manuscripts. "Do you really believe that these ... these things ... have been waiting for someone like you to commune with?"

"No, not at all. Don't you see?" Bernard lifted his chin and scratched at the scruffy beard he had allowed to flourish over the last few weeks. "Look back through history, at all the instances of people who heard disembodied voices. They've always been attributed to angels, demons, gods, ghosts. Those born with the capacity to hear are labeled either saints or psychotics, depending on society's reaction to their story." I had begun to wonder whether Bernard saw himself as a saint or a psychotic, a martyr for science or a madman fixated by an unproven theory, willing to sacrifice integrity and prudence to substantiate a problematic presumption. My lingering skepticism must have been evident. "I've seen that look before, Preston. I know it all too well. I'm used to being called a crackpot, a mad scientist. I wear those monikers proudly. How many researchers over the centuries, on the verge of an important breakthrough, found only derision and disdain from their peers? Be proud to be a part of this. History will remember our names."

That history would record our names, I had little doubt.

How historians would regard our enterprise, however, I dared not consider. Shedding light upon the shadowed spaces of the world often exposed things best left festering in the dark. Blinded by his ravenous thirst for knowledge, Bernard identified his quest as an innocuous pursuit of enlightenment, rejecting any possibility of catastrophic results.

"Every time you try to reassure me, I get a little more spooked." I smiled, masking my apprehension. "I should be getting back. Walid will wonder what has become of me."

"Strange one, Walid." Walid Moawad, the Lebanese linguist assigned to assist me, rarely deviated from the task at hand to socialize. My initial inquiries about his background had been answered courteously but quite curtly. He never spoke of family, friends or how he came to be employed by the institution funding the research. "The company produced him at my request, pulled him out of their back pockets like they had just been waiting for me to ask."

"That's something I've been meaning to ask, about our employers," I began, but seeing Bernard's sudden change of expression, I shelved the question for another time, another place. The oppressive environment in which we worked extracted a severe toll on us as the omnipresent eyes of our patrons scrutinized each step of our progress. Bernard never named those who had resurrected his research, never enlightened me as to their interest in his project or the prospective applications such breakthroughs might engender. He guarded the identity of these silent watchers vigilantly, and with each passing day their impatience proliferated. "Well," I said, defusing the situation, "I was just wondering if I could get a company car."

Another week's worth of work saw the scrolls translated, judged against my edition of *Conversations avec les Morts,* sequenced and methodically examined for discrepancies, correspondences and omissions. Once the 333 stanzas had been properly ordered, Walid read aloud the complete text while Bernard recorded the session.

Regrettably, the touted transmission produced no immediate response. Hours stretched into days, days into weeks. Research continued, halfheartedly, as Bernard scrambled to validate his apparent failure – and to justify my continued involvement in the project.

"Something's missing," he said one evening, sitting at the same picnic bench where he had shared his revelations with me months earlier. Stars diligently occupied their fixed positions, arranging themselves industriously to etch familiar constellations in the darkening heavens. "We're overlooking something. There must be something hidden in the text."

"Something like a code?" By now, Bernard had deteriorated into an animated ghost clinging to the vestiges of fading aspirations. He resembled Hawthorne's archetypal scientist: His beard had thickened and his hair had grown terminally disheveled; his face, lacking any color, appeared ashen and fibrous; angst and apprehension sullied his once focused eyes. Throughout his half-muttered ramblings, his voice cracked with hesitation and self-doubt. "I wouldn't know where to begin."

"All the recordings we have made, all the electronic voice phenomenon we have gathered – there must be a clue there." He gazed skyward, seeking answers from the apathetic twilight. "There are 37 of them – different languages. We can only identify a handful of them, but we know that there are 37 altogether." He paused, eyes darting about in sunken sockets, fingertips tapping against the wooden table top. "Each voice recites a distinct passage nine times. There are 333 stanzas in *Conversations avec les Morts* Nine goes into 333 37 times."

Like gentle ripples traveling across the surface of a secluded pond, I believed the heavens wavered in that instant as dark matter beyond the furthest stars pressed its weight against distant cosmic boundaries. I felt lightheaded and nauseated, felt as though the earth might slip away beneath my feet as some parallel universe collided with our own in a calamitous failure of natural laws.

"I don't think it's a coincidence," I said, watching as puzzle pieces repositioned themselves in my mind's eye. "The ninth word of every 37th stanza, a total of nine words." The revelation poured over my lips though I could not claim to be its lone source. I gave voice to an ancient idea the origin of which I dared not contemplate. "That is the key. That is the invocation we have sought."

Gods and devils of man's construct generally reflect the physical and emotional framework of their creators. Religion and mysticism extend only as far as the imagination of its earthly designers. Science, likewise, finds its limits amidst the most abstract musings of the most progressive and intellectual minds produced by civilization. Glimpsing the wonders and horrors beyond the threshold of human comprehension leads inexorably to lingering fear, paranoia, delusional behavior or complete madness, depending on the degree of exposure.

Nothing that occurred that evening after our unfortunate realization can accurately be conveyed since there is no comparable phenomenon with which to contrast it. Bernard prepared the transmitter as I selected the appropriate words to compose the ancient epitaph. I jotted the words on a steno pad, counting and writing, translating each term as I identified it and hoping that the result would be no more than gibberish. With each successive word, I recognized the pattern emerging and I sank deeper into despair. Instead of eliminating the wild theory, I found myself growing more confident in it.

"Some things are better left undiscovered," I heard myself whisper, repeating my own dire warning. An intangible darkness had settled over the sterile laboratory, insinuating itself into every corner. I felt it churning in my belly, scratching at the inside of my skull. "We ought to stop. We should forget about all this, let it fall back into obscurity."

"Obscurity? It's been waiting for discovery, Preston. We've just tapped into something that was there all along, a natural resource."

Since Walid had retired for the day, I suggested Bernard read the completed phrase. His understanding of Syriac, though limited, would have to suffice for the initial transmission. He held the piece of scrap paper in his shaking hands, stumbling to find the appropriate Aramaic, struggling to remember the proper intonation.

"Hell, I can't do this," he said, and for an instant I thought reason had vanquished his curiosity. His hesitation lasted only moments, though, and an instant later he read the words aloud forgoing the translation. "When the stars align so shall their dark design," he said, and the universe trembled almost imperceptibly.

Although I expected an instantaneous response, I could not begin to fathom the mechanics behind the visual distortions I witnessed over the next few minutes. The very fibers of existence seemed to flutter. Sounds shriveled and light warped. The floor rolled and the walls bowed. Fighting to keep my balance, I watched as a stream of armed guards rushed into the room.

Looking toward Bernard, I saw his lips continuing to move. He realized that he had to follow the set protocol, reciting the nine-word verse nine times. The guards had surrounded him, seemed suddenly eager to incapacitate him. I saw an inexplicable darkness spilling from his head, curling corporeal strands that might be likened to tentacles. A transformation had begun. A passage in the text claims shadows lurk in our hearts; perhaps, the shadows linger in our DNA. When recited in any language, the invocation's catalytic capacity initiates not a transcommunicative response but a physical metamorphosis. I could no longer hear Bernard's voice, but I heard other voices bleeding through from alternate dimensions – voices that whispered a familiar mellifluous mantra. Mercifully, darkness overwhelmed me before the completion of the transmission.

Later, I awoke beneath the retreating darkness just prior to dawn. I found myself outside the electrified fence, resting along the border of the Pisgah National Forest. The facility had been reduced to rubble, and a detachment of soldiers picked through the debris. I smelled smoke and chemicals and some other putrid stench that hinted at burnt flesh. I staggered to my feet and surveyed the ruins from a distance.

"There's not much left," a uniformed officer said, approaching me from a nearby jeep. "Probably for the best. Most of the equipment was stolen. The experiments were unsanctioned and dangerous. You're lucky you made it out alive."

"Have you found anyone else," I asked, though I knew he would not tell me if they had taken Bernard into custody. Perhaps they had apprehended what remained of him, partially transformed into something hideous, something alien and yet rooted in his very cells. "Did you recover anything useful."

"Everything was destroyed by the fire. There were no survivors."

"I don't really remember what happened in there."

"Relax, Mr. Carver, we already know your involvement. We have no intention of holding you responsible for any of this." The officer offered me a cigarette which I thankfully accepted. "Name's Roth. Lieutenant Colonel Mark Roth." He leaned against a towering balsam, watched as his troops began a methodical cleansing of the area. "I joined the service to protect the country against foreign aggressors, to help spread democracy. Instead, I've got to face an invisible enemy with no loyalties, no form and no face," he said, looking toward me as if I could offer some kind of advice. "How am I supposed to do my job, Mr. Carver?"

"Do you hear the voices?"

"All of us hear them," he said, and I knew that Bernard's invention had progressed much further than he had realized. They had shut him down because they were afraid of what he might ultimately discover. They were afraid he might crack the code. "You'll hear them, too, if you don't already. You've been infected – if you can call it that. Damn nanotechnology."

Roth barked a few commands to a group of soldiers who seemed interested in some bits of parchment. The surviving pieces of *Conversations avec les Morts* soon fell to ashes.

"Kirkuk, Baghdad, Damascus, Cairo – there are a groups forming across the Middle East, all over the world, searching for the code to breathe life into these ancient horrors. It's only a matter of time before someone succeeds."

"Do you need help?"

"Every army needs new recruits."

Standing there that morning, watching as Bernard's ill-fated aspirations smoldered beneath a timid spring morning in the Appalachians, I perceived the insistent tug of the universe. All the events leading up to that moment seemed exquisitely orchestrated, predetermined and deftly executed. Even an ostensibly inconsequential creature on an insignificant world had a purpose in the incomprehensible design – a design which only now revealed its paradoxical nature.

In all my studies I had again and again encountered grimoires reiterating the theme of clandestine gates leading to veiled passages connecting the known universe with recondite realities – realms of the preternatural housing horrors beyond reason and imagination, distant cosmic vistas and distorted dimensions sheltering godlike atrocities and servitors of chaos. The physical and spiritual portals mystics had long strived to unlock, however, were the metaphorical reverberations of ancient science and genetic manipulation.

Gone from my nightmares are the horrors from beyond.

Now, I fear the horrors within.

Thy Soul to Him
Thou Servest

Sanford Briggs stepped out of the elevator and into a softly lit corridor on the top floor of the exclusive gulf-front condominium.

He wobbled a bit as he strived for a swift stride, leaning heavily on his stout, brass-tipped blackthorn walking stick. The family heirloom served as more than just a treasured inheritance: Three years earlier, Briggs had suffered multiple fragmentation wounds during Operation Delaware in Vietnam. Doctors who worked with him during his extended convalescence assured him he had been "lucky." Though he did not believe in luck, considering the circumstances, he understood the sentiment.

The hulking doorman scowled as he approached. Briggs expected a less-than-friendly greeting, knowing he had arrived more than three quarters of an hour after the midnight revelries had been scheduled to commence. After inspecting his identification, the sentry grudgingly allowed him to enter the lavish penthouse owned by Giovanni Alvarado.

Inside the great room, socialites and intellectuals drifted amidst shadows as glimmering candelabras illumed ecstatic faces and sparkled upon jewel-clasped throats. The glow of the candlelight scarcely reached the lofty, ornate ceiling, meticulously fashioned in extravagant Gothic style and copiously embellished with intricate carvings of assorted nightmares and grotesqueries. Briggs scanned the panoply only for a moment – he found his admiration curtailed by the disconcerting qualities amongst the tremulous outlines and lurid features of those gargoyle-like shapings.

As his eyes grew accustomed to the dimness, Briggs faltered momentarily as he felt the encumbrance of his own inconsequentiality inhibiting his resolve. The sudden hopelessness that threatened to foil him arose from a powerful spell authored by an adept practitioner of eldritch magick. Briggs promptly shrugged off the hex with a counter curse and merged with the congregation. He hoped he could remain inconspicuous – at least, until the inevitable confrontation made anonymity impossible.

* * *

A few days earlier, Sanford Briggs had been contacted by an acquaintance of the mysterious Giovanni Alvarado. Claiming to have important information about Alvarado's secretive group, he had insisted upon a face-to-face consultation.

The two gentlemen sat upon a green park bench beneath a sprawling live oak, its wide-ranging branches festooned with dangling clusters of Spanish moss swaying in the breeze.

"It is difficult to find someone knowledgeable in all manner of spells and diablerie," the older fellow said. He preferred not to divulge his name. "At least, someone who will readily admit to possessing such knowledge."

"To those who move in the right circles, we are accessible." The younger man's gaze swept the cityscape. A modest Florida metropolis, St. Petersburg had a reputation as a retirement destination. An odd lethargy seemed to permeate the city and its inhabitants. "You apparently move in the right circles."

"Used to," the elderly man said, adamant about clarifying his disassociation from Alvarado's organization. "I used to be a part of that fraternity. No more." He hesitated as he struggled with untold regret and loneliness. His estrangement from the group had taken a visible toll. "I am fortunate to have been a person of little consequence, I suppose. Had I been someone of importance, I might not be here talking with you today."

"You believe the governance of this organization has been compromised?"

"There is a usurper among them," he said, a hint of exasperation in his voice. Briggs also sensed a lingering paranoia, as though the man felt threatened despite his claim of irrelevance. "When I departed, it was evident that things were going in a different direction," he said. He bit his lip, glanced over his shoulder. "A very dangerous direction, indeed."

"If you are not comfortable continuing this conversation, we can meet at a later date," Briggs assured him, worried his trepidation might be justified. The old man shook his head silently, determined to voice his suspicions. "Then, can you be any more specific?"

"As I am quite confident you are aware, there are only two kinds of groups in this discipline." He started rocking back and forth on the bench compulsively. His eyes screwed up tightly and his face grew red and twisted. "One group of worshippers venerates those awful, indescribable entities out of expediency, for the sake of practicality, to ensure through various rituals they are kept from affecting the affairs of humanity and, more importantly, from breaking the ancient binding spells that protect us." The older gentlemen grew more agitated with the utterance of each syllable, as though some transcendent force assailed his mind trying to smother his testimony. "The other type of group actively seeks to establish contact with those same entities, to petition them for aid in their perverse pursuits through the most abhorrent rites ever performed." The old man gasped for enough breath to complete his indictment. "That is what is what will become of the Knights of Sigothaugus unless someone exposes Inanna Gigi Acherontia Waite for what she really is."

A single clap of thunder shook the azure blue skies, startling a family enjoying a midday meal at a nearby picnic table. When the last faint echoes of the sound faded into the distance, one of them noticed that the frail, elderly gentlemen who had been sitting by himself on the bench had suffered some kind of seizure. He lay motionless on the ground beneath the old oak. None of those who came to the man's aid noticed the slight smell of brimstone impregnating the afternoon breeze, the thin ribbons of smoke curling from his nostrils or the strange, muffled tittering of some incorporeal predator.

Nor did anyone notice the 25-year-old man watching the commotion from afar, clutching a sturdy walking stick and mulling the matter over in his mind.

* * *

"I conjure thee, O Creature of Chaos, by Him who removeth the Earth, and maketh it barren." The disembodied voice issuing the invocation did not belong to Alvarado. Somewhere at the far end of the vast assembly hall, the upper ranks of the temple hierarchy encircled a ceremonial altar. The Magister Templi uttered the conjuration while Alvarado, the Ipsissimus, presumably oversaw the ritual. "I conjure thee, that thou burn and torment these undeserving Spirits, so that they may feel it intensely, and that they may be burned eternally by thee."

Briggs carefully navigated the throng of spirited celebrants. Neophytes and inductees congregated in modest clusters along the outskirts, blathering nervously in hushed tones. In some corner, a psychedelic band steeped the room in weird, subdued sounds. The pulsating bass line and tribal percussion attached to the melody evoked Pink Floyd's "Set the Controls for the Heart of the Sun."

Much of the room's furnishings, Briggs reasoned, had been relocated to accommodate those participating in the evening's ceremony. A significant number of adornments, however, remained – perhaps so the owner could flaunt his wealth. Alvarado spared no expense to enrich his Floridian alcazar with rare specimens of high art and priceless antiquities. Recessed gallery lighting showcased his many prizes: On all sides, Briggs observed Chinese terra-cottas, bronzes of Japan, paintings by old masters, tapestries, beautiful rugs, silks, ivories and porcelains along with unique arcana and lesser-known objets d'art crafted by artists whose work bridged the gap between the ordinary and the outré.

As Briggs traced a circuitous route along the periphery, he discerned works by unconventional artists such as Rosaleen Norton, Richard Upton Pickman, Austin Osman Spare, Manuel Orazi and Henry Anthony Wilcox. In a series of built-in custom display cabinets lining one wall, he admired Alvarado's extensive collection of relics plundered from various ancient civilizations – a collection revealing a distinctive concentration on artifacts connected to superstitions and paganism, witchcraft and necromancy, and other facets of esoterica.

One particular piece – an ancient clay tablet purportedly once possessed by Arkham resident and occult scholar Henry Armitage – caused Briggs to linger a moment. The set of inscriptions originated in Alaozar, a legendary city hidden in the jungles of Burma, atop the Plateau of Sung.

"Far out, isn't it?" A young woman approached Briggs with a furtive, cat-like step. She smiled as she presented her hand. "Pardon me, my name is Daisy Parsons."

"Sanford Briggs," he said, his voice no more than a whisper. He hesitated, afraid their exchange might draw attention. Looking around, though, he found the demeanor of the crowd casual and chatty despite the ongoing rite. "Sorry, I'm not really familiar with the etiquette of these functions," he continued, feigning naïveté. "It's rather different than I imagined it would be. How long have you been following Mr. Alvarado?"

"I've been to a few other smaller ceremonies, if that's what you mean," Parsons said. "I'm not what you'd call a 'full-fledged disciple' yet, though," she added, her blithe smile suggesting some degree of indifference. The candlelight gilded her bright face with a golden luster. She wore a black, late-day dress in crepe of acetate and rayon with a v-neck bodice and an attached cummerbund with bow. From her ears dangled jet-colored chandelier earrings of Austrian aurora crystal glass beads set in gold. "All I know is that this is a gas compared to all the weirdness going on in California right now. It's a bad scene out there."

"California attracts all the crazies," Briggs said, hoping his off-the-cuff observation would not offend the young woman. "From what I've read in the papers, there are a lot of charlatans taking advantage of well-meaning people on the West Coast."

In fact, Briggs had poked around a fair share of California-based magical organizations, communes and cults over the last 12 months. Following the Tate and LaBianca murders and the consequent arrest of Charles Manson and his "family," a rash of self-proclaimed messiahs, gurus and spiritualists had set up shop in the Golden State. Some of these fly-by-night sects sponsored abominable acts and encouraged gratuitous sadism amongst their followers. Their very existence brought extra scrutiny to legitimate groups such as the New Reformed Orthodox Order of the Golden Dawn, the Illuminates of Stlottugg and Anton Szandor LaVey's Church of Satan.

"Those are really off the wall, aren't they?" Parsons pointed to an assortment of large Victorian brass lockets, each adorned with engraved floral filigree and suspended from a delicate antique brass chain. Of the dozen samples exhibited, only two revealed their contents: Nestled within each piece of jewelry was what appeared to be an eye. "You don't think they're real, do you?"

"Probably just glass," Briggs said, though he knew that was not the case. He recognized the talismans as 19th century facsimiles of a legendary form of ancient Babylonian amulet which featured an inset preserved human eye, often clasped by sinuous tendrils. Mystics claimed such amulets could be used for scrying and divination. "We may want to continue this conversation a little later," Briggs whispered, nodding toward the center of the room. "Seems as though the main event has begun."

* * *

Earlier that day, Sanford Briggs called upon an old acquaintance in Ybor City, a historic neighborhood in Tampa dating back to the 1880s. Augustine Blackwell, the disheveled proprietor of Brood of Midnight Books, grudgingly agreed to confer with his former benefactor. At first, he denied knowledge of any rumors involving Giovanni Alvarado and the Knights of Sigothaugus.

"Your informant was 78 years old, Mr. Briggs," said the gruff-looking shopkeeper in between bites of a liverwurst sandwich. Mustard oozed out over the rye bread as he continued his noontime meal. "He had a heart condition. His wife passed away last year. What makes you so sure he didn't just die of natural causes?"

"Intuition," Briggs said. "And a name he mentioned, just before something snuffed out his life."

"A name?" Blackwell's exasperation instantly turned into dread. "He gave a name?"

"A woman's name, in fact."

"Don't speak it," Blackwell said, his apprehension mounting. He spilled off the stool behind the cluttered customer service counter and wobbled through the narrow aisle toward the front entrance. He locked the door and drew the blind to shut out prying eyes of customers that rarely visited his establishment. "A woman's name?"

"Yes."

"I do not want to hear it uttered in my presence, do you understand?" Returning to his perch, he rifled through boxes on a nearby shelf until he located a specific amulet on a length of gold chain which he immediately slipped over his head. "That name rouses slumbering things from shadows and echoes through infernal realms filled with ancient horrors. I warned him about her, you know – I ... I shouldn't say any more."

"But you will, Augustine," Briggs said. "If you crossed her, you know you are in danger, too. Tell me what you know so I can end this."

"He took her as his de facto Scarlet Woman, his concubine," Blackwell said. "She claims she was sired by Frater Perdurabo himself, you know. If you ask me, I'd guess she's the offspring of something less human. She's been with him now for almost five years, biding her time."

"To what end?"

"That's the question, isn't it?" Blackwell chuckled nervously. "The Knights of Sigothaugus has undergone a metamorphosis. Most of the old guard is gone, replaced by a younger set of disciples. Some say they were forced out, some say they died of natural causes. The few who point fingers at her, though – well, they don't seem to live very long."

"A bloodless coup?" Briggs had seen similar scenarios play out within secret societies. The threat of such a powerful organization undergoing a complete conversion, however, necessitated action. "The old man seemed to think the Knights of Sigothaugus intended to transfer their alliances, so to speak. Do you believe that to be the case?"

"A decade ago, Alvarado was one of my most reliable clients," Blackwell said. "He would come in once or twice a month and we'd chat all afternoon about this and that. He was sociable, witty and charming. He didn't have a malicious bone in his body."

"That doesn't sound like someone likely to be swayed easily."

"He changed," Blackwell said. "The moment she came into his life, he changed. He financed the construction of Millennium Tower, a 25-story condominium building situated on a private island in Boca Ciega Bay. He began dealing with overseas vendors, importing all kinds of relics and arcana. He distanced himself from former colleagues and embraced some of the more disreputable mystics." Blackwell frowned and shook his head. "If Alvarado walked into my store today, I would not trust him."

* * *

The crowd's deportment had changed. Attendees who had been lighthearted and easygoing an instant earlier now flocked fanatically toward the altar, silent and solemn. The expressions of those nearby grew intent, and their eyes became starry with an eerie enthrallment. The music continued, but its tempo increased progressively, the pace steadily becoming strangely infectious. Briggs could not pinpoint precisely when the chanting began, but once it commenced it quickly engulfed the hall as each participant found the words spilling over their lips cyclically.

Golo stau tha! Gnara lanala! I'atho! Ilalind! Ithathana! Rhauloth r'nac y'gna-egugu!

An uncanny virescent radiance saturated the penthouse, its glow revealing coiling ethereal mists. Briggs had witnessed the same weird porraceous hues on a handful of occasions, most recently at a ritual amidst a circle of megalithic stones atop some unnamed hill in the countryside east of Aylesbury, Mass.

Golo stau tha! Gnara lanala! I'atho! Ilalind! Ithathana! Rhauloth r'nac y'gna-egugu!

The intoxicating mix of chic upmarket perfumes and colognes and the piquant salt spray carried by the gentle sea breeze from the Gulf of Mexico abruptly ebbed, eclipsed by a mephitic, hircine odor. Beneath the droning music and fanatically-mouthed mantra, far more sinister sounds began to ascend from some awful abyss. Briggs, hypersensitive to such phenomena, perceived the contraction of time and the dislodgment of space. He sensed, too, the multifaceted façade that had been erected to keep the participants from seeing the sanity-draining horrors surrounding them.

Golo stau tha! Gnara lanala! I'atho! Ilalind! Ithathana! Rhauloth r'nac y'gna-egugu!

As the more ardent devotees impulsively pushed in toward the altar, a curious spectacle evolved as first one, then another and another participant went sailing into the air, seemingly weightless. Soon, more than a dozen disciples levitated high above the Corian tile floor, arms outstretched and stiff, faces frozen in a disquieting aspect of unsolicited ecstasy. Daisy Parsons might well have joined them in their dreadful rapture if not for Sanford Briggs.

The instant Parsons began to float gracefully toward the other doomed souls, Briggs upended his walking stick and used the cherry scorched derby handle to latch on to the young woman's shoulder, dragging her back down to the floor. She continued chanting, entranced and oblivious to her own rescue. To keep her grounded, he shuffled through a coat pocket until he found a rather lackluster amulet bearing a leafy branch. He hastily fastened the Elder Sign around her neck, hoping no one else had noticed his generous act.

Golo stau tha! Gnara lanala! I'atho! Ilalind! Ithathana! Rhauloth r'nac y'gna-egugu!

Briggs surveyed the quickly deteriorating situation, paying close attention to the soon-to-be-sacrificed lackeys hovering perilously close to the carven figures inhabiting the ornate ceiling. He knew he could not save them. He knew that he had not come to rescue individuals. Briggs had an objective – a specific target. The time for revelations had come.

Golo stau tha! Gnara lanala! I'atho! Ilalind! Ithathana! Rhauloth r'nac y'gna-egugu!

With a tap of his stout, brass-tipped blackthorn walking stick, Briggs tugged at the fabric of the unreality. The treasured inheritance and family heirloom served yet another vital purpose: As the magician's primary supernatural instrument, the luciferous shaft of ancient enchanted wood pulsated with an intense radiance. The effervescent bursts of light emanating from the walking stick obliterated the cleverly-constructed façade, shredding shadow and unveiling the black mass of ravenous monstrosities suspended in the chamber's elaborate Gothic woodwork.

With those assorted nightmares and grotesqueries painfully evident, screams promptly replaced the diabolic incantation, and the gathered assembly – from the diehard disciples down to the most ambivalent neophyte – fled the room in terror.

During the ensuing exodus, the carven figures overhead, now revealed as malevolent preternatural teratisms, feasted upon the helpless floating prey with alarming ferocity. Dark, horrid, alien entities snapped and lunged, claws ripping, tusks goring, teeth gnashing. The things stretched and contorted in the most gruesome postures, exhibiting a nauseating glee in their euphoric frenzy. Their gluttonous howls and shrieks, their bestial bleating and blattering, and their exultant chortling coalesced in an excruciating cacophony.

For ten traumatizing minutes, the carnage continued. Briggs felt the oppressive expanse of the swirling abyss hemorrhaging into his world. The Knights of Sigothaugus had successfully breached the barrier between opposing dimensions, creating a temporary, localized convergence. At its peak, the singularity effectively displaced the corporeal backdrop revealing a startling panorama of galactic necropolises swollen with charred worlds orbiting extinct stars. This celestial charnel house interned unspeakable horrors.

When the tumult finally subsided, Briggs stood alone amidst the tattered bits of flesh and viscera spread across the bloodied Corian tile. Most of the cultists had dispersed, their flight sending many down the darkened condominium stairwell or clambering to squeeze into the elevator at the far end of the corridor. A hurried survey showed a handful had been trampled as they fled – their trodden, twisted bodies lay where they had fallen.

Golo stau tha! Gnara lanala! I'atho! Ilalind! Ithathana! Rhauloth r'nac y'gna-egugu!

A single hooded figure stood before the lavish altar reciting the incantation. Her voice trailed off dreamily, its power and allure intact. From the deep shadows that accumulated in the far end of the room, other preeminent members of the organization – the ranking adepts – materialized. In all, eight Knights of Sigothaugus – each wearing ritualistic regalia – gathered to assess the aftermath of the disrupted ceremony ... and to interrogate the brazen gatecrasher.

Habited in long, dark robes, the practitioners of occult sciences employed masks to conceal their faces.

"Reveal yourself, Inanna Gigi Acherontia Waite." Sanford Briggs issued the demand with confidence and zeal. "Prepare to answer for your transgressions."

"On whose authority do you presume to defile this ceremony and address the Knights of Sigothaugus with such impertinence?" The woman's imperious tone left little doubt as to her identity. She drew back the hood of her vestment, revealing her surprisingly youthful and elegant features. The delicate color in her cheeks, her bright indigo eyes and her soft hair – black as a raven's wing – obscured the viciousness of her soul. "Approach the altar and state your identity."

"My identity is immaterial, and I act on my own authority," Briggs said. He crossed the chamber deliberately, sidestepping discarded bones and circumnavigating vast pools of blood. "Accusations have been levied against you, Inanna Gigi Acherontia Waite. You have been charged with corrupting this organization, and for aligning it with entities known to actively pursue humanity's demise."

Briggs stopped some 20 feet from raised platform upon which the altar, draped in black, rested. He leaned upon his blackthorn walking stick as he studied the shrine's stylized design, with its many ornaments carved in stone, its billowing tapestries depicting scenes of medieval debauchery and heresy, and its prominent mosaic of skulls and bones.

"How do you intend to substantiate your claims?"

"The massacre you initiated here this evening is evidence enough for me."

"Very well," Waite said, her full red lips curling in a wicked smile. "I acknowledge the undertakings of which I stand accused." She stepped forward, her eyes burning with wild intensity. "What you call 'transgressions,' I consider accomplishments. I have revitalized the Knights of Sigothaugus. I have expelled the frail and the feeble, and ejected the benevolent elders who practiced parlor tricks and pontificated on the sacred duty of keeping the Great Old Ones from devouring the universe. In a world that is already rotting from within, there is no logic in shunning such an awesome source of power."

"What about Giovanni Alvarado? Does he share your ambitions? Does he sanction the kind of merciless sacrifice you officiated tonight?"

"Giovanni, my sweet benefactor," she said. "He understands so little of what transpires in these ceremonies. Had you not splintered the façade I created, he would have never witnessed the bloodshed. Even so, he will continue to support me. For an old man like Giovanni, youth is an irresistible incentive."

"No." One of the eight remaining Knights of Sigothaugus stepped forward. His withered hands trembled as he struggled to remove his ceremonial mask. Though Briggs had never met the man, he recognized him at once: Giovanni Alvarado was as frail and gaunt as the elderly man he had met in the park a few days earlier.

Still, the old codger possessed a stubborn soul and great learning, making him a formidable power. "For years, I trusted you. We all trusted you. You betrayed us."

"Betrayed you?" Alvarado's Scarlet Woman took offense at the charge. "I have done exactly what you asked of me when we first met: I have used my powers to extend the lives of your colleagues. And, tonight, I will do the same for you by transferring your consciousness into this man's body."

Waite's admission provided a glimpse of enlightenment. Briggs realized that "the old guard" Blackwell thought had been replaced by "a younger set of disciples" remained an integral part of the organization. The crafty witch had used the collective power of the Knights of Sigothaugus to perform conveyance charms – relocating each member's psyche into a suitable host. Briggs shuddered to guess what had become of the ousted souls.

"No," Alvarado said, his cadence far more livid. "I will not allow it. You said the bodies you chose for us belonged to practitioners of the black arts – those whose actions would directly or indirectly harm humanity. This man has shown it is you who willfully consort with demons and forsaken gods."

"You have no choice, old man," Waite said. "I still have need of your wealth and resources. I will tell you when you are no longer necessary." She had been stalling while she gathered the residual energy from the convergence. She had absorbed so much of the lingering force in the great hall that she glistened with the pallid radiance of distant galaxies. She raised her arms, strangely thin and fragile beneath the fabric of her robe, and uttered a string of cryptic words from some long-dead language. "Da'oshac dha'zacyar ena'ngo! Gyugamit iqugtmis! Logu! Narnoaz O'nthothuguac!"

For a moment, Sanford Briggs found himself back amidst the tall elephant grass in the bottomland of A Shau Valley – a strip of terrain along the border of Vietnam and Laos used as an entry point for supplies being transported along the Ho Chi Minh Trail. Signal Hill – the name

American military personnel had assigned peak of Dong Re Lao Mountain – rose into the hazy infinitude of the hyacinthine sky. Briggs winced as he heard a deafening roar and shivered as the shock wave battered him. He looked down at his leg to find blood and bone, smoldering flesh and fatigues.

Inanna Gigi Acherontia Waite had plucked the episode from his memory and was using it to paralyze him.

Briggs focused his thoughts and steadied his nerves. He began chipping away at the illusion, rejecting its power to encumber him. A wise old British occultist once told him magick was 10 percent skill, 10 percent luck, 10 percent presentation and 70 percent force of will. The chimera rapidly dissipated. Freed from its influence, Briggs retaliated.

He slammed the tip of his blackthorn walking stick against the Corian tile, generating a fiery whirlwind that quickly enveloped the altar. More than half of the Knights of Sigothaugus perished in the opening volley, ill-equipped to protect themselves against the blazing cyclone. In a way, Briggs regretted their deaths, but knew he had little choice.

Before the flames relented, Briggs had conjured a second barrage: With outstretched hand, he beckoned a clutch of chains which sprouted from the floor. The restraints looped and twined about Waite, tightening mercilessly the more she struggled. She shrieked as she fought to free herself before Briggs could cast a devastating spell.

Yitshaki! Thogg! Arllaelli! Yitshaki! Thogg! Arllaelli! Ia! Ia!

Her desperate entreaty seemed to echo through the time and space. Whatever names she had articulated, Briggs sensed her utterance had drawn the attention of an exceedingly powerful force. The Millennium Tower shook on its foundation and the altar cracked, dislodging large shards of marble. Inanna Gigi Acherontia Waite tilted her head upwards and opened her mouth, belching out a caliginous mist which quickly encircled her. When the vapors dispersed, the shackles had vanished.

A swirling vortex appeared in the floor between the combatants, forcing Briggs to retreat several steps back from the platform. The churning emptiness grew more powerful with each passing moment and seemed intent upon devouring everything on the 25th floor of the condominium. Before Briggs could counter the attack, he saw Waite wracked with the brutality of physical transmutation – her infernal collaborator had grown weary of operating behind the scenes and sought to possess the foolish witch. The abject terror in Waite's eyes conveyed her surprise at being dominated by forces she thought she could control.

Her arms became impossibly elongated tentacles which reached across the chamber and coiled about Briggs, crushing him as they pulled him closer to the vortex. Her bright indigo eyes filled with the black barrenness of starless realms. Her youthful and elegant features grew distorted and abhorrent, until the abomination of her deformities could itself engender madness. If any part of Waite remained cognizant, Briggs pitied her.

Briggs fought fruitlessly to free himself. He collapsed, writhing on the floor, sliding slowly toward the vortex. He focused so intently upon his struggle, he failed to notice Giovanni Alvarado had regained his footing on the platform. The old man shambled gracelessly toward the monstrosity that had once been Inanna Gigi Acherontia Waite. It took every ounce of strength he possessed, but he managed to position himself directly behind the ancient horror. Clutching a shard of marble, he raised his hands above his head.

"Blood will I draw on thee, thou art a witch – and straightway give thy soul to him thou servest!" Alvarado plunged the marble dagger into Waite's body, igniting a firestorm that engulfed the entire platform and sent Briggs sailing across the great hall.

* * *

When Sanford Briggs awoke, he found himself resting in the great hall of Giovanni Alvarado's 25th floor penthouse overlooking Boca Ciega Bay. The midday sun spilled into the room through billowing tapestries.

Considering the events of the previous evening, the place seemed surprisingly tidy.

"Good morning."

"Ms. Parsons," Briggs said, only now realizing she had been cradling his head in her lap. "How did – "

"Don't bother asking," she said, patting his forehead. "I can't remember a thing. I woke up in the hallway an hour ago and found the place deserted. Then I saw you, curled up on the floor in the corner."

"Thanks for staying," Briggs said. "I don't know about you, but I'm starving. Do you know where we could get some breakfast?"

"I do, in fact," she said, helping him to his feet. "Oh, I found this." She handed him the remains of his walking stick. In addition to being split in three pieces, it appeared to have been charred. "I'm sorry it broke. You can lean on me, though."

Briggs silently accepted her offer. He had earned the right to a little generosity.

* * *

Several hours after the last guests had departed, a grave-like stillness settled over Giovanni Alvarado's penthouse.

The Knights of Sigothaugus had ceased to exist and the owner of the luxury condominium would most likely never again be seen. His disappearance would undoubtedly become a much-discussed unsolved mystery that would perplex both investigative authorities and future seekers of arcane lore.

Eventually, someone would come to inventory his possessions and to liquidate his many valuable assets. On this afternoon, however, the penthouse remained empty. Therefore, no one noticed that one of the large Victorian brass lockets, adorned with engraved floral filigree and suspended from a delicate antique brass chain, began to vibrate within the glass-encased display case in which it rested. No one noticed when, like two of its twins, its locket unfastened and it opened to reveal its contents.

Daisy Parsons knew something was amiss from the moment she awoke from the nightmare. In her dream, someone had ousted her from her body, leaving her adrift in some bleak limbo. Now, she felt formless and insignificant, like a spectral patch of lingering consciousness with no means of communication. She recognized her surroundings, but she could not shift her gaze. She could not even feel her body.

In that ephemeral moment between the realization of her fate and the crippling insanity which ensued, Daisy Parsons would have screamed had she a mouth to express her horror; would have shattered the glass had she hands with which to strike; and would have fled had she legs to carry her.

Instead, she silently wept in that awful grave-like stillness.

Upon an Altar in the Fields

1.

    Midnight had passed by the time Churchill Gardener reached the edge of the lagoon, but the starry night furnished sufficient radiance to guide his cautious footsteps.
    The vastness and brilliance of the twilight sky hypnotized him with the sweep of boundless constellations. In his fever-fueled euphoria, the unbroken heavens felt strangely accessible, as if the doorway to a corridor leading to distant and unknown vistas might suddenly be revealed in this remote milieu. Stubbornly, he strived to dismiss such notions, attributing his foolishness to lingering delirium.
    He had come this far, though – and not merely out of scientific inquisitiveness.
    Gardener warily approached the water's edge. Amidst the mangroves that partially encircle the broad bay, Gardener sensed unexpected movement. He felt his hand – still wrapped in bandages – reach into his pants pocket. When his fingers made contact with the cold, smooth stone, the darkness filled with the sound of drums and tramping feet.
    He froze for a moment, struck by the sudden revelation that he had successfully escaped his mundane existence. His emancipation, however, might well cost him his life – or his sanity. Like everything else on this picturesque Caribbean island, the glassy, starlit waters of Salt River Bay took advantage of inherent natural beauty to shroud dark and disturbing secrets.
    When he first arrived in St. Croix, Gardener's objectives had seemed much less complicated.

2.

"Put that away, man." The young Crucian shuddered as if some disturbing thought had been dislodged from his memory. "It is not something meant to be displayed in public."

Churchill Gardener obligingly slipped the small, rectangular stone tablet back into to a leather drawstring pouch and returned it to the safety of his pants pocket. The curious relic – one of more than a dozen such tablets that had been donated to the Peabody Museum – measured roughly 4 inches by 5 inches and featured a series of inscribed dot-patterns that defied translation. He carried with him two examples.

"I beg your pardon, sir," Gardener said, speaking as reassuringly as he could. He surveyed the bustling crowd in the morning marketplace and found no evidence to suggest anyone had taken any interest in the incident. "I was unaware of its offensiveness. In fact, I am hoping to find out more about it. You seem to recognize it – can you tell me what it is?"

The man glared at Gardener with a cold, contemptuous indignation. Like most inhabitants of this island, he could undoubtedly trace his lineage back to the waves of African slaves transported aboard Danish and Dutch vessels and sold to wealthy plantation owners as free labor. For nearly two centuries, generations faced the injustice of endless drudgery and brutal captivity toiling in the sugarcane fields. The death of that ghastly industry came with the abolition of slavery in 1848, brought on by a fiery rebellion that saw many plantation estate houses burned to the ground.

Yet Gardener sensed that the African-Caribbean islander's disdain had little to do with the treatment of his ancestors. The stone had provoked some dormant fear and aroused his suspicions.

"My grandmother called them 'summoning stones.' I only know that it is a bad thing, something one does not possess unless they intend to do harm or bring about suffering and pain," he said. His sudden uneasiness stood out in sharp contrast to the gracious demeanor of other vendors with whom Gardener had spoken at the Frederiksted market. "It is an evil omen from times past, but for some it still carries great power."

"I can assure you that it is nothing more than a stone with some atypical inscriptions," Gardener said. "Perhaps you may know of another merchant here at the market who might specialize in this sort of thing?" The lively bazaar bubbled with a certain Old World charm, evoking pangs of nostalgia as Crucian peddlers touted all manner of locally-grown produce, from papayas and mangos to carrots, tomatoes and yams. A few fellows offered salted fish alongside grinning children who hoped to earn a few coins selling the beautiful tropical shells they had collected. Here and there, older sellers hawked artifacts found amidst the ruins of once palatial Danish manor houses. "I would be willing to compensate you for any information that might help me learn more about this little stone."

"Even in a place such as this, so tranquil and unspoiled in the eyes of outsiders, there is danger in asking the wrong kinds of questions," the man said. "Now, please, go on about your business. If you have any sense, you would rid yourself of that thing before it causes you grief."

Reluctantly, Gardener acquiesced, thanking the man for his time and shuffling back into the crowd. He tried to convince himself that he should be satisfied with the knowledge that he was on the right track. Since his arrival on the island a day earlier, none of his inquiries had generated a hint of curiosity in the stone tablet, let alone the kind of clear recognition this young Crucian had demonstrated. Still, he sought more than circumstantial justification for his fact-finding mission – he needed to find someone who could help solve the mystery.

His investigation had begun a few months ago when Lily Buhrman approached the collections director at Peabody Museum in Cambridge, Massachusetts, and offered to donate a small collection of Carib Indian artifacts. Buhrman, a nurse, helped set up the first municipal hospitals in St. Croix after the United States paid Denmark $25 million for her holdings in the West Indies almost a dozen years earlier, in 1917, renaming them the U.S. Virgin Islands. Buhrman had accumulated the pieces gradually, accepting them from local residents as gifts of gratitude for her services. Much of the assortment consisted of stone, bone, ivory, shell and earthenware objects along with pictograph inscriptions upon serpentinite – all desirable pieces, though generally not considered uncommon or extraordinary.

The presence of 17 greenstone tablets, however, caused a great deal of conversation and conjecture at the museum. Nothing comparable had ever been recovered in the Caribbean. The untranslatable dot-patterns inscribed upon the stone had no parallel in the Americas. At least one noted Assyriologist likened it to rudimentary cuneiform scripts from remote sites in Mesopotamia. An analysis by Miskatonic University's Professor Warren Rice argued that the impressions bore a striking resemblance to an ancient civilization along Africa's Gold Coast. Upon a few of the stones, pictograms complemented the script, each image depicting grotesque combinations of real and imaginary creatures – some whimsical and farfetched, others frightening and yet oddly familiar on a primitive level.

Gardener – a professor of natural science and distinguished archaeologist – had convinced his superiors in the Department of Anthropology at Harvard University to send him to the Caribbean island of St. Croix to ascertain the origin of the mysterious stone tablets. He had argued with as much passion and earnestness as reason, though he did not confess that his request had as much to do with his own personal interests as it did with the pursuit of knowledge.

Gardener, at age 58, believed that he had become as obsolete as the ancient artifacts he spent decades scrutinizing and cataloging. He had done his share of field work early in his career, but the responsibilities of academic tenure had kept him chained to a desk for as long as he could remember. His occupation had become a sepulcher: Where the study of ancient civilization once provided him a passage to far-flung destinations, now it offered only the constant reminder that – as empires perish and kings fade from memory – the inconsequential lives of common men and women are quickly lost to time.

He made his journey aboard a vessel owned by the Quebec Steamship Company, sailing out of New York. The ship made port in St. Thomas before anchoring in the harbor at Frederiksted in St. Croix. After dropping off cargo and passengers – ferried to shore in a frenzied procession of smaller crafts – the steamer continued on to Demerara in British Guiana on the northern coast of South America.

Frederiksted had precious few guesthouses; fortunately, the island attracted even fewer tourists, particularly in late summer. Gardener managed to find a vacancy at the first inn he visited, an unpretentious affair situated on one of the narrow lanes near the wharf. Like its neighbors, the building's architecture incorporated the Victorian styles of the era in which it had been built. Though Frederiksted dated back to 1751, plantation workers had torched much of the town in 1878 during a labor revolt, leading to its reconstruction.

Having spent much of the morning browsing the vendors' wares in the marketplace, Gardener returned to his temporary residence to find the small, six-table dining area in the courtyard preparing for an anticipated rush of lunchtime patrons that seemed unlikely – although the building boasted the only visible Coca-Cola signage he had seen on the town's main thoroughfare.

"Just a cup of tea for now," he said as he took a seat. The waiter – a lean and lanky islander with square shoulders and a noble countenance – nodded so casually that Gardener could not be certain he had heard his request. After the server lingered a few moments longer, Gardener repeated himself. "We can discuss your menu options in a few minutes."

"Very good, sir."

"Don't mind him." The voice came from a tall, dignified man standing near the garden gate. "Deaf in one ear, poor man. Best to face him when speaking – he understands every word so long as he can see your lips moving." Clean-shaven and tastefully attired, he offered a genial smile with his salutation. "Name's Julian Ramsay. I heard that I had some company from the states – didn't much believe it until now."

"Churchill Gardener." He stood and welcomed the fellow American with a handshake. "Word gets around. I only arrived yesterday. Please, join me for lunch."

Ramsay promptly agreed and, after Gardener had explained the purpose of his visit, he offered his services as a guide around St. Croix.

"I've been here for a few weeks now and I'm beginning to feel like a native," Ramsay said. "I'm on assignment, currently with the American Geographical Society, writing sketches of the Caribbean islands. I started out in Trinidad nearly two years ago and I've been working my way north and west, hopping from island to island, village to village. I pick up stories wherever I can find them. Most of my articles go to the society for their various publications. Some I sell to other publications through my agent in New York."

"Where else have your articles appeared?"

"Depends upon the content," Ramsay explained with a broad grin. "Anything from U.S. daily newspapers to pulp magazines and specialty press journals. The latter, though not well known, have proven to be some of my most lucrative markets. Some of them you may recognize, but most are quite obscure and target a limited readership. I'll name a few – tell me if anything rings a bell: *Bizarre Destinations, Modern Biologist, Savage Realms, Wicked Worship ...*"

"I'm afraid I haven't heard of a single one, Mr. Ramsay," Gardener said. "Regardless, I do believe that I will accept your offer of a guided tour. When shall we begin?"

"As soon as you would like." At that moment, the friendly waiter appeared at their table with two piping hot bowls of chowder. "Well, as soon as you would like after we enjoy lunch, at any rate."

The midday meal consisted of a stew containing old wife fish and vegetables served with plantains and a dumpling made from cornmeal and okra. When Gardener asked the waiter to give his compliments to the chef, the Crucian laughed and said his wife would be pleased.

"Mind if I have a look at that stone you mentioned," Ramsay asked, his curiosity whetted. "I don't have any background in your chosen field, but I have seen my share of pottery shards and Indian bric-a-brac over the last few years."

"Certainly." Gardener removed one of two leather drawstring pouches from his pocket and placed its contents on the table. "This is what petrified the vendor in the market this morning."

"This is rather remarkable, isn't it?" Ramsay's eyes squinted as he studied the stone's peculiar inscription. "No wonder it caused him such dismay. There's something ominous about it, wouldn't you say? Something that hints at tribal ceremonies and witchcraft."

"I think you may be reading as much into it as he did," Gardener said. "These Crucians are predisposed to superstition. They seem to follow a hodgepodge of dissimilar traditions, with no visible separation between Christian doctrine and the folklore handed down from their African ancestors."

"I see no conflict of interest, to be honest." Ramsay leaned back in his chair and watched as a crowd shuffled into the small establishment. "What harm can come from incorporating myths and legends into an imposed form of religion? We should all be so bold as to customize our convictions."

From their uniforms, Ramsay knew the men worked with the Virgin Islands Agricultural Experiment Station run by the U.S. Department of Agriculture. One among them came forward and negotiated with the owner over how to accommodate the entourage. For a moment, Gardener thought he discerned a glint of recognition in Ramsay's eyes, as though he might be about to hail one of the members of the lunch party. Whatever caused the impression quickly evaporated, leaving in its wake an awkward interlude in their conversation.

"Well, as one with no inclination to any form of religion, I cannot argue with that." Gardener, realizing that their table would soon be required, placed several bills upon the table – far more than necessary, but far less than he would have paid for a comparable meal in Boston. "I suppose my aversion to religion makes my contempt for superstition that much more severe. I sometimes wonder if civilization will ever evolve beyond its innate fear of shadows."

"Religion and superstition aside, sometimes there is reason to fear the shadows," Ramsay said. He took another look at the stone, examining it closely. "Sometimes, there is reason to fear those who are drawn to things that dwell in darkness." He hesitated for a moment, wrestling with some unspoken disinclination. Whatever reservations he had slowly evaporated. "I believe I know what caused your friend in the market to react with such abject terror. I have seen markings like these. They are found in a place that holds painful memories for the Crucians."

"Why didn't you say so, man? You must take me there at once!" The urgency and tautness in Gardener's voice betrayed a note of intellectual impatience more fitting a novice. "All this worry over legend and folklore – I am sure there is nothing to fear. Can we visit this site today? Can we go there now?"

"Yes, but please understand: I cannot guarantee your safety," Ramsay said. "This may be American soil, but it is a far cry from your snug office in Harvard. You will see that the vendor's fear was more than justified."

3.

Although only 15 miles separated the two most populated cities on St. Croix, it took more than two hours to make the short trip from Frederiksted to Christiansted in a Chevrolet Superior Roadster. Julian Ramsay rented the vehicle from the owner of Richard Hansen & Co., one of the island's most successful business concerns. The company imported lumber and building supplies while simultaneously exporting sugar and other local products.

Churchill Gardener appreciated Ramsay's proposal to show him the island's landmarks, but frequent detours through small, impoverished villages along the poorly maintained Center Line Road had him wondering if they would ever reach their destination. He endured his host's loquacious history lessons, his musings on the future of the rum industry in light of the U.S. prohibition on alcohol and a series of quaint anecdotes about Crucian customs.

The afternoon had begun to wane when they finally reached the roofless ruin of a once sprawling estate outside Christiansted. According to Ramsay, Richmond Hall survived the 1848 rebellion but fell to flames in the 1878 labor riots locals called the Fireburn.

"Like many other European families, the owners chose to cut their losses, fleeing the island with whatever possessions they could carry," he explained as he searched for a suitable spot to park the car just outside the main house. "Whatever property remained became fair game for Crucian subsistence farmers who carved out patches of land from the abandoned plantation." He paused, searching the landscape as if worried that others might be watching them. "This is the place," Ramsay said. He somehow managed to stow a Coleman Quick-Lite lantern in the cramped two-seater. "We'll need this. The chamber where I saw markings like those on your stone is located beneath the remains of the sugar mill just this side of the cane fields. It was used as one of many storage vaults in years of peak production; this one, though, sometimes served a more appalling purpose – before the emancipation of the slaves."

A torture chamber – though he dared not utter the terrible words, Gardener knew instinctively that the undercroft had likely doubled as a makeshift dungeon where disobedient slaves had faced incomprehensible cruelties. If his lifelong studies of civilization had demonstrated one irrefutable fact, it was that man's capacity for inhumanity to his fellow man never diminishes.

Upon entering the shadowy vault, Gardener immediately appreciated the angst that had overcome the market vendor that morning. In the darkness, he saw shackles and chains and a grisly assortment of instruments designed to inflict pain. No amount of objective analysis could ever determine the precise number of souls that endured odious abuses within these walls. No scientific instrument could adequately gauge the scope of their anguish.

Between the warm glow of Ramsay's lantern and the thin beams of sunlight pouring through a small gap in the wall near the chamber's ceiling, Gardner could clearly see the inscriptions etched into the stone blocks. The hopelessness of his surroundings smothered any elation he might have otherwise enjoyed. Had the smile that often accompanied an important discovery threatened to blossom across his face, he would have surely stifled it.

"I haven't come across anything like this on any other island," Ramsay said. "I believe that it is unique to St. Croix – and I think that there is a good chance that the slaves imprisoned here were responsible for covering the walls with this script."

"This is fascinating – tragic, but fascinating," Gardener said. "I will need to document this, even if it takes all night."

"No – you mustn't stay after dark," Ramsay said. "I have a small camera in the two-seater. It's probably not as good as the kind you are used to, but it should suffice. I'll get it."

"Wait," Gardener said, his hand clutching Ramsay's arm. "I can understand how this place would evoke great fear among the descendants of slaves. It is a direct connection to their history here. But what are you afraid of? What here causes you so much apprehension?"

Despite his youthfulness and vigor, Ramsay's expression betrayed a faint look of distress. Ever since departing Frederiksted, Gardener had detected some lurking dread, some unspoken worry that his new acquaintance sought to conceal with his rambling roadside lectures.

"Remember how I said that people who consort with things in the shadows should be avoided at all cost?" Ramsay's eyes involuntarily glanced toward the gap in the chamber wall, sweeping the weedy expanse between the crumbling mill and the ruined manse. "There are rumors of a cult on the island, its members keen to restore some of the island's more brutal qualities. They immerse themselves in shadow and replicate rituals once practiced by Danish plantation owners – ceremonies centering on the worship of some pagan fertility god."

"Men of power always seek to dominate through acts of terror," Gardener said. "The mere rumor of these ceremonies can cause worry and unrest. Have you spoken to the authorities? If there is evidence of some cult, I am certain an investigation – "

"The authorities may well be involved," Ramsay said. "It is best that we work quickly. Let me fetch the camera so you can get started."

Ramsay departed without another word, leaving the lantern so that Gardener could explore the adjoining subterranean chambers. The archaeologist stumbled through more than a dozen networked rooms, each haunted by shadows and clammy dankness. Here and there, he came across some centuries-old artifact: a rotting wooden crate and assorted bits of machinery once used to for crushing cane into juice; stray pieces of furniture from the manor house, spared from flames due to disrepair; and a modest desk upon which rested a set of ledgers long ignored.

Gardener also discovered a small cache of portraits secreted in a storage area. He imagined the owners of the plantation, faced with the likelihood of violence during the Fireburn, scrambling through the manor hoping to save a few precious belongings. That the authors of such institutional injustice could not foresee the inevitable consequence of their actions both mystified and sickened him. That same strain of chronic shortsightedness still poisoned various segments of the population.

More than an hour slipped away as Gardener explored the interconnected vaults of the plantation. Only when he returned to the makeshift torture chamber did he realize how much time had elapsed – and that Ramsay had never returned with the camera. By now, the sun had fallen below the horizon. As the last of the day's radiance exited the sky, Gardener realized that he faced the night alone.

Except ...

He saw them marching hurriedly through the gathering gloom, following the same route he had taken with Ramsay earlier that evening. Enveloped in thick black cloaks with hoods drawn over their faces to ensure anonymity, they carried blazing torches and scythes. They moved with disciplined precision and purpose as if animated by fervent devotion.

Gardener had no doubt that the participants in this nocturnal procession were those Ramsay had accused of being active cultists. He doused the lantern, hoping to observe whatever ritual they intended to perform. His inquisitiveness still outweighed any irrational fears that might be forming.

The group formed a ring around a stone slab on the edge of the neglected sugar cane fields. In the next moment, a chorus of masculine voices, dire and guttural, combined their lugubrious tones to produce an abhorrent howl. The slurred, half-incomprehensible torrent of utterances and intonations that followed lacked meaning, but something about it seemed blatantly malevolent.

When one of the hooded brethren led Ramsay – stripped of his clothing, beaten and bloodied – to the sacrificial altar, Gardener had only an instant to estimate the extent of his own growing distress. Seconds later, fear seemed too feeble a word to describe his emotional state.

The cultists closed in on the altar, their murderous scythes rising and falling, hacking and stabbing. The blades, shimmering in starlight, grew slick with blood and gore. Throughout the prolonged carnage, the clustered zealots repeated their chant – *Mek'eggne dhagaca chaatho in the fields where dwells the goddess! Gogosthorua mosk g'otloile Sakength Nugganoth! May this blood sustain her!*

Gardener felt a sudden searing pain in his right leg. He plunged his hand into his pocket, retrieving the two pouches containing the greenstone tablets. While one remained dormant, its twin pulsed with preternatural energy. Dumping the relic onto the floor, Gardener found it glowing with inexplicable heat, as if plucked from the fires of a forge. It smoldered for a few seconds before transmuting into a small pile of ashes.

At that moment, Gardener noticed that the cultists had abruptly ended their invocation. In place of it, he now heard only screams. Gazing through that narrow gap, he saw something moving in the cane fields – something the cultists had apparently not expected. A few of them backed away slowly from the altar while two or three ran shrieking into the night. Most lingered near the gruesome carnage that had been Ramsay.

My grandmother called them 'summoning stones.' What had seemed an unimportant declaration that morning now caused an acknowledgement of the unfathomable forces behind this nightmare.

The cultists stood in awe as they entity they inadvertently summoned emerged from the fields. From his vantage point, Gardener could see only a vast, amorphous mass, its undulating translucent hide speckled with bulbous, darting eyes. From beneath its bulk sprouted countless serpentine tendrils that scuttled across the clearing with startling swiftness. At first, the wormy appendages sought to claim the corpse splayed upon the ancient altar in the fields. That token of appeasement, however, left it unsatisfied.

One by one, the cultists, too, fell victim to the god of their misguided adoration.

Gardener turned away as the massacre intensified. He fell to his knees and wept. He felt strangely violated and vulnerable. His understanding of the world had been utterly invalidated. He did not know if he would survive the experience; he did not know if he wanted to go on living having been forced to look upon what lurks in the shadows.

When the first tendrils slipped through the gap in the wall and sought his flesh, Gardener scampered through the darkness.

My God, Gardener thought just before losing consciousness. *It burns. It burns.*

4.

When Churchill Gardener awoke – mercifully extricated from an endless showcase of horrific nightmares – waves of pain immediately assailed him. Every extremity ached. Every inch of his flesh smoldered. Every bone stung and every organ throbbed.

His vision cleared gradually and he found himself in a small, unfamiliar room. The bare walls, thatch roof and dirt floor provided enough evidence for him to make an educated guess: He was in a Crucian home in some humble, out-of-the-way village. His ears caught the sound of the surf, placing him near the coast.

"To tell you the truth, I didn't expect you to wake up, friend."

Gardener sought the source of the voice. He found his elderly caretaker seated in chair in a corner of the room. The Crucian smiled and nodded.

"How did I get here?"

"I found you wandering along the road several miles outside of Christiansted," he explained. "I had no way to get you to the hospital, so I brought you to my home and did my best to care for you. I keep hoping someone from the city will pass through so I can send for medical help. Some of your wounds aren't – well, there isn't much more I can do for you."

Gardener tried to shift his weight and roll onto his side but the resulting agony nearly caused him to black out again. The most excruciating pain originated in his lower left arm and traveled up to his shoulder and across his chest. He lifted his head enough to take inventory of his injuries. He found an array deep scratches and punctures. A few carefully placed bandages concealed what may have been even more severe damage. Whatever remained of his left hand had been tightly swathed in grimy rags bound with twine.

Upon seeing his condition, all of his senses suddenly seemed to sharpen. With his regained lucidity, he became aware of an overpowering stench: gangrene.

"What is your name?"

"Ulmont Kettle."

"Call me Churchill, Ulmont." Somehow, Gardener managed to sit up and swing his legs over the side of the cot. "How long have I been here?"

"About a week, Churchill." Kettle offered him a cup of brownish water which Gardener accepted gratefully. "May I ask you sir: What happened to you?"

"I'm not sure that you would believe me if I told you, Ulmont," Gardener said. "I'm not even sure I can explain it. I went to the ruins of Richmond Hall and something ... something hideous came out of the fields." Gardener trembled uncontrollably as he recalled the event. "It devoured my friend Julian. It killed all those men, its own worshippers. I think it came because of the stone." Gardener's right hand patted his pants pocket but found it empty. "It's gone. I had this small greenstone tablet."

"The summoning stone – I have it, here," Kettle said, retrieving it from a box on a bedside table. "Wherever did you find it? I thought these had been lost over the years."

"I am sorry to say that I brought it with me to St. Croix," Gardener said. "It was donated to a museum in America. I came here to learn more about it. I wish I had never seen it. I had no idea that it was a source of such evil."

"You are mistaken," Kettle said. "The summoning stone is neither good nor bad. It is simply a key which unlocks a variety of doors. Behind some doors lurk treacherous gods and ancient horrors; behind others may be found benign beings and benevolent entities." Kettle returned the summoning stone to its owner. "It is said that one such doorway may be found not far from here, in a cove west of Christiansted. One need only go to the shore, place the stone in the water and wait. A three-masted white schooner will appear and its captain will extend an invitation for an endless voyage."

"If only such tales were true," Gardener said. He stood, surprised he could summon up the fortitude to overlook his pain. Knowing that his chances at survival now seemed slim, he asked for as much paper as they old man could find along with pen or pencil. "Let me put my thoughts to paper, just in case anyone should come looking for me. I need to tell them not to question my sanity and to heed my words should they ever visit the ruins of Richmond Hall."

* * *

Midnight had swept passed and the white light of the moon shimmered on the waters of Salt River Bay.

Churchill Gardener had managed to hike more than a mile through the darkness. He imagined an impatient avatar of Death pursuing him down the sandy path to the beach, along the coastline and into the thicket of mangroves. He felt life slipping away with each step, with each raspy breath and with each twinge of pain.

That he had allowed Ulmont Kettle to talk him into such a foolish endeavor underscored the severity of his fever-fueled euphoria. Recent events had forced Gardener to reshape his perception of the universe – to concede that unimaginable forces could intersect the inconsequential lives of common men and women and, purposely or accidentally, make them a bit more relevant in the Grand Scheme of all things known and unknowable. Still, Gardener held out little hope.

When he placed the summoning stone into the water the entire lagoon glowed with an uncanny luminescence.

"You see," Kettle said. "I told you."

"You said there would be a ship."

The three-masted schooner glided in from the open sea, its course taking her directly over the reef and several feet above the surface of the water. It came to rest near the mouth of the bay, close enough that it could lower a plank into the shallow surf and welcome two new passengers aboard.

Their youth restored and their wounds healed, Gardener and Kettle set sail that night for the city of Celephaïs on the Cerenerian Sea, home of the turquoise temple of Nath-Horthath and the street of pillars.

Defector

A weary, lonely, paunchy pensioner sat in a yogic position, meditating on the dimming stars of distant constellations swirling in a vast vortex projected on the wall of his cramped apartment.

The vivid spectacle harkened back to an age of seers and oracles which mainstream 20th century science had systematically marginalized. Nevertheless, the same sciences which scorned all things esoteric and arcane saturated and stimulated all magical arts, as evidenced by the peculiar jumble of electronics and vacuum tubes and convex lenses which promulgated the cryptic display.

As he viewed the manifestation, the man sensed considerable cosmic agitation. Unseen, unknowable forces with reprehensible designs scuffled amidst the great gulfs of nothingness at the edges of universe, willfully aligning themselves in preparation for some cataclysmic conflict that could ultimately threaten a multitude of universes.

The Englishman had encountered individual entities of unimaginable power during his lifetime, had communicated with Things That Must Not Be Named and collaborated with omniscient horrors found in the Great Abyss. In all his years, though, he had never felt so many eyes turned back upon him. Never before had he felt so diminutive, so inconsequential and meaningless.

Then, all else withered as one presence eclipsed whole galaxies. Beneath its awful gaze, countless worlds perished and pulsing stars failed. The Englishman immediately recognized Thoth's appalling avatar, the hideous monstrosity known as the Thing in the Yellow Mask.

Something had captured its attention. Something had drawn its terrible stare. As it slowly peeled back its façade, the Englishman shuddered at the revelation churning in his crimson-tinged eyes.

His eyes opened and the image shattered, gradually fragmenting into small, fluttering eddies that faded out of existence.

Unsettled by the vision, the Englishman had few options. He wasted little time making the arrangements. The Elders would convene within hours.

* * *

As tradition demanded, the Elders met at an old tavern situated on the northeast corner of the intersection of two cobblestone avenues in an unremarkable New England town. Though they dwelt in remote corners of the globe, knowledge of certain portals allowed near instantaneous travel from continent to continent.

The Wayward Witch Inn originally opened its doors in 1795, though prior to that a public house had stood on the same grounds, its name lost to history. The original building suffered heavy damages in a fire in 1844 and, with generous monetary contributions from a number of secretive fraternal organizations, the owner rebuilt. Aside from the Prohibition years, the tavern had been operating continuously since the 1840s – and for those in the know, the owner continued to conduct limited business surreptitiously as a highly exclusive speakeasy through the 1920s.

Since the repeal of the Eighteenth Amendment, the establishment had resumed full operations, and, taking into account the ailing economy, had managed to maintain a modest margin of profit. Continued endowments from the same enigmatic associations ensured sustained revenue.

The Englishman represented one of those esoteric societies which frequently donated funds to maintain the bastion secreted within the building.

He arrived before the others, a newspaper tucked beneath his arm as he entered the establishment. He found the pub vacant save for the current owner's unsightly daughter who sneered at him when he opted for black coffee over a pint of stout.

The old man – bald and plump and riddled with scars from a lifetime of excess – settled into an uncomfortable ladder-back chair in a back room overrun with shadows that may well have dated back to colonial times. His brittle bones snapped as he tried to relax. From his pocket, he withdrew a Roman denarius depicting Emperor Claudius. He began flipping the ancient coin between his fingers rhythmically.

The daily's headlines screamed "war." Adolph Hitler's army had managed to crush all organized resistance in Poland within a matter of weeks. His Luftwaffe hammered cities; panzer divisions swept across the landscape and artillery pounded fortified positions into so much rubble. For the most part, the world did little more than hold its breath. There had been declarations of war, with prime ministers rattling swords and grumbling stern cautionary words; but no military power could reach out and repulse this first audacious incursion by a despotic German totalitarian.

More importantly, no one could prevent the atrocities that would surely follow.

The Englishman had been active during the Great War, gathering information for British intelligence agencies and participating in acts of espionage and artful assassinations. His involvement remained a secret – his government preferred to manipulate the public's perception of the eccentric mystic, feeding the press sensationalistic rumors and dubbing him "Pawn of the Devil" and "the Great Blasphemer" – appellations he neither embraced nor disavowed. The only designation he vigorously rejected was "wizard."

While he remained an operational representative of the Secret Intelligence Service's top secret Chimera Section, the Englishman still considered himself a freelance occultist and ceremonial magician.

Henry Hoffmann Smith, the Englishman's sanctioned American counterpart, slipped into the main room without being observed by the owner's daughter. He checked his pocket watch as he strolled across the polished wooden floor, his footfalls oddly silenced. The meeting had been set for noon – he had arrived a few minutes early.

"You've gotten long in the tooth, old man," Smith said, claiming a seat directly across from him at the oaken table. Smith, tall and lean, led a relatively cloistered lifestyle, working on perilous capers behind the scenes as directed by a clandestine branch of the American military. "Your keepers aren't going to let you retire in luxury."

"I possess everything I require," the Englishman said, his voice monotone. His piercing eyes burned into the American's skull. The considerable powers he once wielded may have ebbed, but his charisma remained potent. "I am comfortable."

"At least they're feeding you well – or do they make you earn your keep doing those magnificent parlor tricks you've mastered over the years?" Smith smirked as he assessed his rival's corpulence. Continuing in his best Cockney accent, "All bangers and mash and kidney pie, guv'na?"

"I am delighted that you can have not allowed all the ominous auguries to diminish your fondness for droll banter, Mr. Smith." The Englishman's solemnity and his stern, somber glare underscored his disapproval. "Or perhaps you have failed to notice that Europe is about to descend into the maelstrom once more. I do hope you Yanks join in the fray a bit earlier this time around. You certainly sat on your hands until the bitter end last time."

"The situation is being monitored, closely," Smith said, repeating a snippet from his most recent policy briefing. "It takes time to convince the isolationists even when war is inevitable. Americans aren't too keen on sending their sons to foreign shores to fight – particularly when they feel far removed from the enemy."

"The Poles probably thought they were safe, too," the Englishman said. "Talk to them now that they are being driven out of their homes at gunpoint. They have the honor of digging their own graves."

As the two continued their exchange, others began filing into the Wayward Witch Inn. The new arrivals boasted such exotic dress and striking ethnicity that it was immediately evident that none called New England home. Their ranks included a Chilean Kalku, a Seid from

Normandy, a Bruja from Argentina and a Hamatsa ritualist from British Columbia.

The barmaid continued to exhibit a less-than-friendly air when serving the visitors, though their appearance had no visible effect upon her. Their arrival neither surprised nor stunned her. The inn had served as a sanctuary for such gatherings for centuries; in her lifetime, she had seen far stranger things pass through the doors of the tavern. She knew enough not ask questions, not to refuse a direct request and not to disclose information about the congregation to any outsiders. Doing so could nullify the lucrative covenant her ancestors struck.

"I hope this was necessary," said the Norman Seid. André Guignery, a portly, elderly gentleman with small puffy eyes and a sagging silver mustache, shambled close to the table as he addressed the Englishman. His trembling voice overshadowed his light French accent. "Traversing the Ethereal Corridors brings undo attention. The Germans are working on technology that will allow them to map the multiverse conduits. Their agents have been seen poking around the Erdeven dolmens, the Kerzerho alignments and the Necropolis of Bougon."

"Bloody Schäfer and the Ahnenerbe have the country's top occultists tromping all over Tibet searching for Leng," the Englishman said, his loathing palpable. "Can you imagine that: A team of Hitler's scraping young errand boys blindly fumbling around in the snow hoping to stumble on a fissure in the dimensional threshold?"

"Whether he knows it or not, Ernst is sharing his skull with some peripheral entity," Guignery said, confirming various intelligence reports suggesting members of the Nazi hierarchy might be under the influence of malevolent forces. Cerebral manipulation – synonymous with what the Catholic church defined as demonic possession – had been used to change the course of human history. "Himmler probably provided the medium."

"Gentlemen," Smith said, his impatience suddenly noticeable, "we should continue this discussion in the back." A handful of locals had wandered in looking for a midday meal and a dusty mug of lager. "I don't think these townsfolk have any interest in a discourse on metaphysical physics."

The six attendees stood simultaneously and – with Smith leading – marched back by the bar without uttering a single word to barkeep before walking single-file down a narrow corridor. Passing restrooms and several doorways leading to stockrooms or storage closets on either side, Smith stopped when he reached the end of hall and faced an array of framed, hand-drawn scenes dating back more than a century. At face value, the sketches detailed pioneer life in the small New England town, depicting various pastoral scenes.

Something in their construct, though, seemed amiss – the artist's hand had crafted uncanny angles and skewed foreshortening to create a highly distorted perspective. To the casual viewer, the want of symmetry and the monstrosity of misproportion remained inconspicuous. To one who dared hold the etchings to higher scrutiny, however, the perversion of their composition threatened madness.

For Smith, the disequilibrium generated by staring at any one of the images caused momentary lightheadedness and a rush of giddiness. Immune to the sanity-warping effects of the images, he had experienced similar phenomenon on countless occasions and had traversed this very corridor at least a dozen times, triggering the cryptic force majeure. As intended, staring at the sketch gradually realigned his faculties, revealing a hidden aperture in the corner of the hallway – an opening little more than a crevice.

"Put a hand on the shoulder of the person in front of you and close your eyes," Smith said. He slipped through the passage easily, leading the others into a hidden chamber. To anyone unfortunate enough to observe the procession, the group would appear to be walking through a solid wall.

To onlookers, the event would appear to be orchestrated by magic.

The Vault had been established in the early 19th century as a sanctuary for mystics and magicians, seers and soothsayers and alchemists and occultists. The hexagonal chamber could comfortably hold a dozen congregants. The attendees took seats around a three-section, Chippendale banquet table dating to 1790. Adorning the otherwise bare walls, portraits of former guests included Ciro Formisano, Fulcanelli, Johan August Strindberg, Thomas Lake Harris, William Woodman, Eliphas Levi, Gerard Encausse and Hargrave Jennings.

There on the table, Smith had already set up a most peculiar apparatus consisting of a shallow, oval-shaped silver platter in something akin to a well-and-tree design (though the tree had been replaced by the jagged branches of the indomitable Elder Sign) connected by cables to one six-volt lead-acid accumulator, a nine-volt electrolytic dry-cell battery and another 120-volt dry-cell.

"It's based on the Teslascope," Smith said with more than a hint of giddiness, "although the lodge boys call it a 'hyperdimensional transceiver.'" He rarely made an effort to muffle his pride in American ingenuity. Smith made a few minor adjustments, spinning dials and flicking gauges and jostling cables. "Of course, poor Nikola is under the delusion he's been chatting with civilized beings on Mars and Venus all these years. That isn't quite the case."

"I did not realize that you Yanks had explored this form of evocation," the Englishman said. "Radiomancy is still in its infancy in London."

"Oh, we've done more than explore it, old chap," Smith said, winking sardonically. "We've outright mastered it." The American took out a Scottish ceremonial knife, a sgian dubh, and opened the flesh of his left thumb. He placed his hand an inch above the platter so that drops of blood fell into one of the branches of the Elder Sign. "Who's next," he asked, wiping the blade on his pant leg. "Nothing to it."

"Perhaps someone would care to bring the rest of us up to speed," Guignery said. "Other than the obvious political issues facing Europe at the moment, I am not entirely clear what circumstances led to this meeting."

"The Englishman here believes he saw a boogeyman," Smith said, handing the blade to the Argentinean. "The lodge boys apparently concur, or they wouldn't have lent me their favorite toy."

"Ancient shadows are stirring," said the Bruja Mamerto Manuel de Rosas, wincing as he slit his thumb. "I've had visions of strange man cloaked behind a yellow veil standing beneath a black moon."

"Bad signs, bad stars," the Hamatsa ritualist added, his voice gravelly. He knew only a smattering of English, and sometimes used terms from his native Kwakwala tongue when unable to find the proper word. "Night brings a black makwala."

"As it turns out, the Office of Naval Intelligence provided some information that may explain the sudden unwelcome interest of our long-distance voyeur." Smith – his left hand still hovering above the platter – retrieved a grainy photograph of a German ship. "The Panzerschiff *Undine*, under the command of Capt. Reinhardt von Eichhorn, has sunk 22 allied merchant ships and three armed merchant cruisers in less than two months. By comparison, a sister pocket battleship, the *Admiral Graf Spee* sank only nine merchant ships in the same time period.

"The *Undine* sailed from Wilhelmshaven and within hours was witnessed traversing the Mozambique channel. Similar disparities have arisen, essentially putting this ship in two different oceans at virtually the same moment." Smith paused as the knife passed to the final participant in the evocation. The Englishman glared at the blade momentarily before proceeding to make the cut. "We believe the ship is utilizing the Niflheim Channels to travel great distances in mere moments."

Far older than the Ethereal Corridors and capable of accommodating larger trekkers, the Niflheim Channels had been constructed by an unknown race long before mankind's earliest ancestors roamed the Earth. Metaphysical physicists speculated that they were only a small component of a much larger network which stretched throughout the universe, a complex system so extensive that those who originally orchestrated it had likely forgotten how to navigate its more remote sectors.

"They must be using a pulse repetition summoning to invoke an astral aperture, probably slaughtering their captives as a catalyst," the Englishman said. "No need for a prison ship. All the victims they pluck from the seas end up as sacrificial mechanisms to drive the reality inversion."

"At first, we suspected its magnitude was dependent upon the sacrificial transmutation of power derived from prolonged suffering," Smith said. "The math didn't add up until we realized they were amplifying the power using a Yithian crystal."

"If that is the case," the Englishman said, reaching across the table to return Smith's sgian dubh, "each transit has the potential to rouse extraterrestrial entities."

"Worse," Smith countered. "We have reason to believe the ship's captain, Capt. Reinhardt von Eichhorn, a known member of both the Kult des Namenlosen and the Reich des Schwarzen Mondes, may be trawling for allies in the Great Abyss."

"The fools do not know what kind of power they are dealing with," Guignery said. "If Hitler's Kriegsmarine opens the door, there will be no hope for any of us. How do you intend to put an end to this operation?"

"We've struck a bargain with a known Friendly," Smith said, referring to one of the entities sequestered in the infernal realm which had previously shown compassion for humanity. "This evocation will bind it – the combined will of six Elders should be sufficient enough to control it. We've already instructed it to capture the *Undine*. We have calculated the time and place when the ship will next use the Niflheim Channels. In fact, we have less than an hour."

"Then let us begin," the Englishman said.

"Everyone must place their hands upon the platter," Smith said. "A word of warning: Once the connection is made, removing your hand will most likely result in instant death. We've lost a few good agents at the lodge that way."

A few moments later, the walls of the hexagonal chamber vanished, replaced by the utter blackness of deep space – a seemingly endless dusk dotted by tiny clusters of pathetic radiance that comprised distant galaxies. On the very edges of perception squirmed a host of unspeakable entities.

Nearby, the Friendly squatted on the charred moon of some dead world, its thousand eyes studying the Elders with unequivocal apathy. Its flailing tentacles lashed at the twilight as it spat spidery nightmares from its gaping maw.

* * *

The Elders waited patiently for 57 minutes.

As Smith had predicted, the *Undine* slipped into the Niflheim Channels, appearing suddenly in the haunting dusk, sailing as if still cutting through Atlantic swells. Even as the Englishman channeled his thoughts into the Friendly, urging it to immediate action, he wondered whether the vessel sought only to make use of the conduit as a shortcut to its next high-seas target or if its captain hoped to secure an alliance with one of the terrible entities of the Black Abyss.

He also wondered how Smith had managed to calculate the precise coordinates and the exact time of the transit.

Before the Friendly had lifted one tentacle, the spectacle broadcast by Smith's contraption quietly faded. The endless twilight was replaced by the six walls of the chamber. The *Undine* disappeared completely, its fate unknown.

The Englishman immediately realized Smith had vacated his seat. Turning to his left, he beheld a grisly scene: Each of his colleagues sat motionless, blood spurting from gaping wounds in their throats.

Before the Englishman could react, he felt a cold sensation beneath his chin.

"Sorry, old boy," Smith said, drawing the blade quickly from ear to ear. He chuckled when he felt warm blood gush over his hand. "You brought this on yourself, though. You shouldn't have been poking around my corner of the cosmos."

The Englishman leaned back and directed his gaze upward into Smith's face. There, he saw the crimson-tinged eyes of the Thing in the Yellow Mask. When Smith had become its pawn he could not know any more than he could speculate on whether the American had Nazi sympathies or merely sought power for himself.

Still, he had all the evidence he needed: Smith had become a turncoat, collaborating with the same of malevolent forces hastening the Nazi agenda.

The weary, lonely, paunchy pensioner jumped out of his chair and spun around on his heels, driving the blade of the sgian dubh deep into the defector's chest. The American's eyes widened as pain mingled with shock. Smith looked first at the Englishman and then to the other Elders. To his astonishment, he found the injuries he believed he had inflicted had been part of an elaborate illusion.

As he fought for breath, Smith gazed into the hand he believed held the ceremonial knife. There, he found a very old coin – a denarius depicting Emperor Claudius.

"Parlor tricks," Smith said, choking on a mouthful of blood. He slumped forward as Thing in the Yellow Mask abandoned him.

* * *

Several days after the Elders convened, Capt. Reinhardt von Eichhorn of the Panzerschiff *Undine* was visited at sea by a strange old man, bald and plump and riddled with scars from a lifetime of excess. He awoke from the encounter as if from some terrible nightmare.

The first mate managed to transmit a distress call before he joined the rest of the bridge crew in an ever-widening pool of blood. The call put the ship about 100 miles off the Argentine coast.

According to the Kriegsmarine, the *Undine* sank in heavy seas. All crew members were lost.

Izothaugnol Ascending

1.

In 1947, Bernard Baruch called it a "Cold War," a clash of ideals and principles confined to rhetoric, propaganda and aggressive diplomacy. By the time I got involved, the war was anything but cold. Skirmishes simmered in Southeast Asia, Central America, the Caribbean and in European countries just outside the Iron Curtain. Both sides employed assassination, espionage, brutal intimidation and deliberate acts of state-sponsored terrorism to coerce developing countries into alliances.

And sometimes, the Cold War spilled over into a much older conflict.

My name is Sydney Weldon Vaughn. It would be misleading to say I was an agent for the United States. I worked for an organization ostensibly conceived of by faceless Pentagon patriots, funded by private individuals and corporations with neither national nor philosophical allegiances. Once established, the institution gradually detached itself from oversight and became a kind of elitist cabal, influencing both American and Soviet politics and preventing either superpower from gaining an inequitable advantage.

In late 1961, we were just beginning to get our house in order. The world had its problems. Any day it could unthread itself, unravel into utter crawling chaos – a fate that would have amused more than a few distant spectators.

"We're at war," deputy director Eugene Bowman said, sitting on a bench on Park Avenue within walking distance of Grand Central Terminal. The lofty octagonal Pan-American building cast a long shadow. "We're not doing so well."

"The Reds are gaining momentum in this hemisphere, thanks to Castro," I said. I remember my first meeting with Bowman, thinking I had forfeited a promising military career to fight Communists in covert operations. He cleared things up that early Sunday morning.

"I'm not talking about that war, Sydney," he said, handing me a dossier. "I'm talking about something that has plagued civilization for centuries. I'm talking about external forces of unimaginable power, lingering just outside of our casual awareness, beyond our diluted senses."

"Sir?"

"Right now, all you need to know is that everything you believe is a façade, a delusion constructed to obscure the horrors of existence and the ultimate insignificance of civilization. A dark engine drives us all, Sydney, and only through vigilance and measured revolution can we hope to end the silent subjugation of the human race."

"Yes, sir." He spoke in riddles, revealing enough to win my interest without naming names or outlining strategies.

"I need you in São Paulo," he said, standing. The briefing had concluded. My first assignment I would find detailed in the documents he had provided. "Maintain your focus. There will be distractions, things you may consider important, but you have a specific objective. You'll learn on the job. I have faith in you. You're a good soldier."

"Thank you, sir."

"Now, wait three minutes and follow me. See that drug store on the corner?" I followed his gaze and nodded. "Give this to the man inside," Bowman said, handing me a slip of paper. "It's a prescription. That's the only place you'll want to go to get it filled. Won't cost you a cent."

Bowman walked off down the uncharacteristically empty New York City sidewalk. He was Old Guard, a veteran of the Second World War, Pacific Theater. Well into his fifties, he displayed no frailties of advancing age aside from a receding hairline and a slight limp that impeded his otherwise steady gait.

In a moment, he disappeared through the front door of the pharmacy, never looking back over his shoulder.

Three minutes later I followed.

Inside, I found no sign of Bowman. The undersized establishment displayed no more than two aisles of medicines including cold remedies, cough syrups and various vitamin supplements. A young man wearing oblong glasses with thick, black frames stood behind the counter. His hair was short, boot-camp style.

"Can I help you?"

I placed the paper prescription on the wooden countertop.

"Yes, sir." He reached beneath the counter and retrieved a small, black bottle. "Have you used these eye drops before?" I shook my head, examining it. "Once daily, in the morning as soon as you get up. One drop into each eye, preferably in a dark room. Don't rub your eyes afterward, don't wash them out. You may tear up a bit. You may get a mild headache."

"What is it for, exactly?"

"It improves your vision," he said, smiling. "More accurately, it enhances it. It contains a substance that stimulates the pineal gland. The substance is cumulative. Once you've finished that bottle, the change will be permanent."

Not fully understanding his explanation, I thanked him and went on my way.

I returned to my apartment, examined the dossier Bowman had assigned to me. Transportation and lodging had been arranged. I would leave the following morning, departing from LaGuardia. Following several layovers, I would arrive in Congonhas, take a taxi into the city, check in at a little hostel in one of the city's older neighborhoods and await further instructions.

Before leaving the next morning, I sat in my darkened studio apartment, tilted my head and, for the first time in my life, I opened my eyes.

2.

São Paulo, even in 1961, was a study in contrasting cultures. Modern skyscrapers like the Jaragua Building towered like arrogant gods over quaint old streets and buildings that dated back 400 years. The wealthiest Paulistas maintained palatial residences, their riches derived from thriving coffee empires. Meanwhile, impoverished families lived in wretched slums crawling with vermin and tainted by dark despair and resentment.

As horrible as those miserable barrios may have seemed, I saw things far worse in the days following my arrival in Brazil.

Had Bowman not forewarned me, I might have questioned my own sanity. After the second application of the prescribed eye drops, the real world began to expose itself. I can only describe the initial feeling as one of creeping despondency. Natural beauty, under new light, revealed its inherent flaws while the uglier aspects of life became increasingly hideous.

I recognized for the first time that things are not always what they seemed to be; people are not always who they seemed to be. I saw the things that walk among us. Many remained superficially human even to my chemically expanded senses – constructed or bred to be less conspicuous, to infiltrate society and to instigate chaos. Among this class, the Shadow Whisperers were most numerous. With glowing crimson eyes and sickly yellow flesh, they slipped unnoticed through crowds of people, always mumbling, always muttering, implanting seeds of fear, distrust and animosity.

They are the source of the insidious paranoia that became endemic in the second half of the 20th century.

Peeling back the grubby curtain and peering out the window, I saw them weaving through the crowded marketplace in the streets below, things that should have existed only in the shadows of nightmares walking transparently amongst townsfolk in the middle of the day.

"You're Vaughn, right?" My Brazilian contact found me cowering in my cramped dwelling a few days after my arrival in the city, still wrestling with the effects of the drug. "Taking your eye drops like a good guerrero, si?"

"Yeah."

"Bueno, señor." He sat at the foot of the bed, threw me a hand kerchief to mop the sweat on my face. "You'll get used to it. Doesn't take long. My name is Gaspar, by the way," he said, introducing himself. "You're in good hands, here. The caretakers are sympathetic to the cause. They understand."

"Agents?"

"No, just plain folk," he shook his head. "Not everyone needs the eye drops to see what's out there. Some people have naturally heightened senses. Call it intuition, clairvoyance, extrasensory perception or sixth sense."

"How can they handle it?"

"Most don't. Most end up in asylums." Even though my exposure up to that point had been limited, I remember thinking that insanity might be less disconcerting than acceptance. "Poor bastards, no one believes them – but they're right, and the rest of the world is blind."

"Where do they come from?"

"Oh, they've been here all along. We've just gotten better at recognizing them." From his build and his manner, I could tell he was only a few years my senior, but he wore his worries on his face. Whatever hardships and heartbreaks he had suffered had aged him prematurely. Gaunt and gangly, his skin was darkly tanned like a rolled cigar. His eyes retreated into dark, burnished pits. Once, he may have been handsome. Seeing those things had eroded his features, worn away at his veneer. "Generally, coexistence is viable – even beneficial in some ways. Occasionally, something steps over the line, usually by invitation. A situation arises, and we must step in and put things right."

"Balance the scales?"

"Precisely."

"And that's why I've been sent here," I said, dismissing a wave of nausea. "I'm supposed to assassinate one of those things."

"Well, you can try, but I wouldn't put my cruzeiros on you." He chuckled but the smile evaporated quickly. "By our standards, these things are practically immortal and virtually invincible. Slow 'em down a little, sure. Kill 'em – good look, it's your funeral."

"Then what – why was I brought here?"

Gaspar stood, searched his pockets. He took out and unfolded a grainy black and white surveillance photo of a burly middle-aged man wearing an unbuttoned, long-sleeve shirt. The picture had been taken from a distance and showed the man addressing a group of native Brazilians in an outdoor setting, possibly a village in the jungle. I recognized him immediately.

"You're familiar with Maximilian Vogel, si? He goes by the name Mueller now, Luca Mueller."

"Yes." My assignment began to make sense. I had helped the American military ferret out former Nazis in the last few years, taken part in cooperative manhunts with the British and Israelis. Some subjects were terminated, some brought to trial. One I smuggled back to the United States after faking his death – I had been ordered to return him so that he could be persuaded to serve the American government. "He's here? In São Paulo?"

"In Santos, actually, about forty miles from here," He said, gazing out the window. His initial friendliness began to dissipate, replaced by growing unease and anxiety. He scanned the streets below, searching for something. "We must complete our business rápidamente, señor."

"What does he have to do with all this?" Vogel, a notorious war criminal and former Nazi, had committed acts of singular degeneracy and depravity so appalling that even some of his contemporaries branded him a butcher. Fürchtegott and Verschuer labeled his experiments grotesque and "of dubious scientific value," but never lifted a finger to halt them. Only Matthias Batsdorff, another infamous Nazi butcher parading as a scientist, supported his so-called research – terrifying and pointless tests performed on gypsies that amounted to nothing more than torture. "Has he formed some kind of alliance with those things?"

"Worse," Gaspar said. "He's managed to stir a powerful being, provoked him into ending centuries of dormancy and rekindled his inclination for worship and sacrifice. Tonight," he continued, "he'll attempt a ceremony that will allow Izothaugnol to exploit weaknesses in barriers that have kept him from physically returning to earth."

"He can control this thing?"

"Of course not, but he thinks he can. They always think they can control them."

Gaspar cautiously retraced his steps, backing away toward the door. Sensing my confusion, he gestured toward the window and I warily surveyed the scene. "We've got company."

Wearing tan uniforms, three men marched through the crowd defiantly eyeing the natives with embedded loathing. Blond-haired, blue-eyed constructs of fabled eugenics experiments, these men had come for me – to make sure I never came close to finding Vogel. As if to provide evidence of their collaboration with those "exterior forces" Bowman had mentioned, a hoard of hovering monstrosities followed their lead.

Gaspar motioned toward the door as he pulled out a Ballester Molina M1916, an Argentine clone of a Colt M1911 .45 caliber.

"What are those things?" Looking like winged, black caterpillars, each creature had a four long, spindly spider-like legs protruding from the spot where its eyes should have been. Beneath the grasping appendages was a puckered, ovular mouth lined with thorny teeth.

"A Seething Swarm," Gaspar said, flinching. "You've heard of our piranha? Same principle, only less friendly and airborne."

Instants later, machinegun fire echoed through the old hostel, generating a torrent of screams from frightened townsfolk in the street. Without hesitation, I grabbed my gear and prepared to follow Gaspar.

"Got a weapon?"

"I thought you said you can't kill them."

"*Sí*," he said, smiling. "But you can kill zealots."

3.

In our exodus from São Paulo we left a grisly mess at the hostel – one the local authorities would be forced to unravel or conceal. Gaspar may have been well-informed and instinctive, but he possessed wretchedly deficient shooting skills. Vogel's men had already infiltrated the establishment's first floor, and we found them in the long hallway leading from the front to the back door.

Gaspar scattered several indiscriminate shots down the corridor, most of them ending up embedded in the walls and ceiling.

"Sorry señor. I'm much better with a machete."

Brandishing German MP 35 submachine guns – a favorite of Hitler's elite Waffen SS during the war – Vogel's assassins began a systematic sweep of the first floor. Having alerted the death squad to our presence, we had no choice but to finish the job quickly and efficiently. Though no words were exchanged between us, it became evident that Gaspar expected me to handle things.

After finding adequate cover for my gun-shy acquaintance, I drew my Walther P38K and put all three down with little effort.

The Seething Swarm dispersed upon their demise, deprived of direction. Sadly, the keepers of the hostel had already fallen victim to them – we found their remains in a pile of bloody bones in the office. Another ten guests had been gunned down in the melee, and the sirens of approaching policia bemoaned the carnage.

We managed to slip out into the streets of São Paulo unnoticed.

On the two hour drive to Santos, speeding down some 2,500 feet on winding roads, along hairpin turns and across chasm-spanning bridges, Gaspar initiated me into this new world. According to him, Izothaugnol was a Great Old One, a member of an extraterrestrial, hyper-dimensional race that colonized earth long before the rise of sentient life. He explained as much of the history as he thought I could manage given my naïveté in the field.

"Most recently, Izothaugnol had worshippers in the Xingu region, indigenous peoples that performed elaborate ceremonies well into this century. The Juruna recognize it as an elemental force but do not deify it like other tribes." He said that in stone carvings, Izothaugnol had been depicted as seven intertwined serpents with a single head, twenty-one eyes and a mouth ringed by tentacles bristling with needle-like quills. Regional folklore suggest that he can reverse the flow of the seasons, and at least one European grimoire attributes to him the power to transport acolytes through time portals. "His cult center was based in Goiania, until Vogel moved it to Santos."

"But if Izothaugnol cannot physically appear, how did the natives learn to worship it?"

"Good question. It communicates with select individuals through dreams. The natives consider sleep to be a kind of temporary death, and dreams are another world, separate from this. In that world, Izothaugnol can connect with them."

"What about Vogel? How did he end up here?"

"Why do you think so many Nazis fled to South America? Look around you." In the dense forest lining the steep terrain on either side of the roadway, I saw ancient shrines not visible to the untrained eye. Upon an adjacent hilltop I recognized a step pyramid all but reclaimed by nature, its crowning altar long abandoned and thirsty for blood. "They came not only to escape prosecution." Many war criminals – particularly the so-called academicians – were known to have dabbled in the occult, mixing science and magic and exploring arcane lore and eldritch teachings. "They came here to continue their work, to put themselves in a position to communicate with dark forces."

Skeletons of ancient, wicked cities dotted the jungles, imperceptible to the ordinary people but excruciatingly evident to one with enhanced powers of perception. Shielded from detection by sophisticated alien technology or residual psychic energies, Gaspar explained that the ruins harbor horrors unspeakable – things that may well reemerge over the coming decades as the reckless pursuit of natural resources pushes plunderers deeper into the wilderness and the borders of rain forest continue to contract.

"Vogel and the others exploited the mythology of the indigenous peoples to establish a new religion." A decade and a half of manhunts had led to developing countries where pagan worship flourished in remote areas. My own experience tracking war criminals left me without a doubt. I began to connect the dots. Certain members of the Nazi elite had specialized in plundering Europe's libraries, museums and private collections, appropriating relics and gathering esoteric literature. "These men always had a hidden agenda. They didn't care which side won the war – they just wanted to divert attention from their own actions."

"Now you're catching on," Gaspar nodded.

I realized my previous ignorance kept me blissfully oblivious. History became a tangled sequence of lies and half-truths, religions a prop, philosophy a distraction. Like darkness visible, the shadows plaguing our progress, prodding us into unwanted wars and rampant nationalism and ethnocentrism became as clear as the veiled entities stalking us.

"If they challenge us, how can we mount a defense?" I turned to Gaspar, who returned my blank stare. "If they already control us, how can we hope to stage a successful rebellion?"

"Destiny, some say, is written in the stars," Gaspar said. He pointed toward the eastern horizon, the band of purple hovering above the Atlantic heralding nightfall. "Their powers ebb and flow like the cyclic tides. Until the stars are right, they cannot recapture their former dominion. They can only influence civilization, obstruct us from achieving our potential before they reunite."

The early signs of dusk had begun permeating the skies as we approached the seaport of Santos. As the distant stars emerged like celestial candles illuminated by unseen hands in the cathedral of twilight, I gazed skyward momentarily transfixed by the vastness of the cosmos. Tiny points of sparkling light crowded the night sky, falsely portraying a universe teeming with life. In reality and by our own technological standards, the great abyss of vacuous space and dark matter made each galaxy an inaccessible atoll, each individual star an isolated island. In that immeasurable void, earth was but a speck of dust.

Driving down streets centuries old, through a city settled less than a hundred years after Columbus sailed, we proceeded in uncanny silence. Gaspar had revealed as much as he could. I had resigned myself to the hopeless crusade.

We approached the darkened harbor, parked alongside an immense warehouse. By day, tobacco, bananas, processed sugar, rubber and coffee flowed through this busy port, traveling to America, Europe, Asia and Africa.

Dockside, we found a group of men – brothers of those we had left for dead in São Paulo – standing guard outside a derelict tanker. The shadows concealed other less tangible sentries, things my eyes strained to detect. I followed Gaspar as he found adequate cover behind a mountain of crates. On deck, a single silhouette leaned against the ship's railing.

"That's Vogel," I whispered, but Gaspar lifted a hand to silence me.

I heard the squeal of tires on the pavement before I saw the headlights. A car sped into the shipyard, screeching to a standstill on the other side of the crates only yards from where we had hidden.

Vogel shambled down the gangplank, approached the vehicle tentatively. One man stepped out of the car, facing the war criminal. With his back to us, I could not identify him. Following abridged salutations, a brief conversation ensued. The car's engine muffled their voices burying the substance of their heated dialogue, though

Vogel's spirited gestures and dissatisfied scowl attested to a bitter and apparently escalating disagreement between the two men.

"This is unexpected," Gaspar said softly. "And unfortunate."

"Do you know who the other man is?"

"I have an idea."

Vogel snapped his finger and all of his guards scrambled, lining up in formation behind him. Vogel stepped to one side. A torrent of machinegun fire cut the seven fanatical servants down where they stood.

"I can kill them both from here,"

"Not yet – the ceremony has already begun," Gaspar said, frowning. His face seemed clouded with disappointment, his eyes flooded with unshed tears. "We go through life thinking we shape destiny, when really we only play roles we were born to play."

The man from the car looked over his shoulder, scanned the darkness where we crouched. My fingers teased the cold steel of my sidearm. His face remained concealed, cloaked by a black veil. Turning back to Vogel, he produced a shining cylindrical object from his pocket – a translucent, pulsing shaft that resembled polished quartz but possessed an almost alien aspect.

Vogel held out his hands, his palms upturned. He gazed upon the object with a mix of ecstatic reverence and maniacal anticipation. I think he may have giggled, overcome with rapturous bliss and exhilaration.

Behind them, the bodies of the men began to transform. As shadow retreated from the growing luminosity of the object, their forms elongated and softened, their features melted into memory. Their limbs merged and their bodies distended and undulated unnaturally, and their flesh reformed as snakeskin.

A sphere of light now expanded from Vogel's cupped hands, radiated outward, swallowing the car, the crates and the bow of the ship. At its center, I saw a serpent's head, I saw Izothaugnol forming, fusing with seven writhing bodies squirming in the shipyard.

The man wearing the veil backed away from Vogel, away from the dock.

"You see the object Vogel is holding? In a minute, he'll disappear – at that moment, I need you to shoot that thing – shatter it into a million pieces. I will handle Vogel – it is more important that you destroy the object." Gaspar wept openly now. At the time, I thought he feared the ceremony had gone too far – that he could not stop Izothaugnol from returning. Machete in hand, he leaned forward, readying himself for an action I could not have anticipated. "You are a good guerrero, señor." He tucked a slip of paper in my shirt pocket, patted me on the shoulder. "Prove me wrong. Find a way to change destiny."

Gaspar charged into the pulsing light, tackling Vogel. The men instantly vanished.

"Gaspar!" I screamed, abandoning my cover. The crimson eyes of Izothaugnol glared at me, its seven tails thrashing with fervent life. Ignoring its hypnotic gaze, I took aim and fired. A single shot ran out, and the shining cylindrical object burst into a shower of glittering shards, like millions of shimmering stars almost frozen in time, descending and slowly fading.

Izothaugnol evaporated instantly, unable to complete his materialization, banished again from this world and forced into exile to await the next invitation. Its premature departure preempted the hideous metamorphosis that would have provided its seven serpentine bodies, leaving behind the dying forms of seven men combined into one shuddering and bleeding mass. With seven mouths it screamed, and its shriek will echo through my mind until death mercifully dismisses it.

4.

Days later I found myself in a little library in the town of Santos. The events that had transpired had been reported as a multiple homicide. Speculation leaned toward smugglers. Investigators had no leads.

The black-veiled man had disappeared. I never discovered his identity.

The slip of paper Gaspar had deposited in my pocket stated the name of the library and included a file number. I approached the reference desk casually, placed the piece of paper on the countertop.

"Por favor?" The woman behind the counter smiled and nodded.

A few minutes later she returned with a copy of a local newspaper. Not knowing exactly what to look for, I thanked her and retired to a table in an empty corner of the building where I could examine the periodical uninterrupted.

Dated late September, 1939, I scanned the headlines. Much of the front section detailed recent events in Europe, devoted to coverage of Germany's invasion of Poland and annexation of Danzig. World War II had begun.

I found what I was looking for buried in the second section. An unnamed man had been shot to death by local police after he was found crouching over the mutilated body of a foreigner near the docks. An artist's sketch of the victim and suspect accompanied the story.

In return for summoning Izothaugnol, Vogel had arranged to go back in time, perhaps thinking he could alter the outcome of the war. Izothaugnol had obliged his whim. Armed with foreknowledge, Gaspar kept Vogel from achieving his objective.

Gaspar had circled his picture. He left a message for me, too.

"Vogel won't get a second chance. History can't be rewritten. It's up to you to find out if the future is equally inflexible."

Unconvinced that my continued service would have any impact on the fate of civilization, I still carried out my duties for the next several decades, serving mankind's best interests to the best of my knowledge. I strived to live up to Gaspar's challenge, hoping to find evidence that we are not simply executing predetermined actions like puppets with unseen masters.

As I near the end of my limited immortality, having faced the unmasked horrors of this world, I still cannot resolve one mystery. I would like to believe my life was my own.

    Staring into the cathedral of twilight, watching as the celestial candles slowly burn away toward the great blackness at the end of time, I pray that I am not a mere cog in an invisible machine driven by some dark engine I cannot hope to comprehend.

The Breach

1.

TAHLEQUAH, N.C. – Administration officials at William Whitley College announced this week that the science department has been awarded a substantial grant by C-Right Inc. Department chairman Dr. Ranier Nordhaus plans to refurbish sections of the vacated Life Sciences building on the north side of the campus. He hopes to modernize the school's harmonics research facility.

"My hopes are to make William Whitely College a leader in the field of theoretical physics, working with other institutions and organizations toward a better understanding of the universe through research and investigation into contemporary conjecture including the String Field Theory."

From the *Haywood County Register*

2.

"You can see it, can't you?" Harley Saunders could not tear his gaze from the sparkling radiance bathing the far wall of the university lab. The sealed environment crackled with electrostatic energy, flooding the room on the opposite side of the shatterproof window with sporadic bursts of light. "You're recording this, right?"

"Yeah, yeah." Randy Moody scratched notes on a legal pad, the sharpened tip of his pencil ripping the cheap paper. His glasses remained perched on the end of his nose as his eyes pulsed with a combination of excitement and trepidation. He glanced at the closed circuit monitors, verifying the decades-old cameras captured the phenomenon. "Blast shield? Lower it?"

"Yes," Harley said, noticing the coffee in his mug had begun to tremble. Instinctively, he rested his palm against the Formica counter – he could feel it quake beneath his touch. Not good. Harmonic energy was radiating outside the boundaries of the test area. "No, wait" he said, scrambling for his cell phone. "Let me call Dr. Nordhaus, he should be here for this." Harley's fingers fumbled with the keypad. "I can't get a signal." The phone's display scrolled with a jumble of unrecognizable characters – digital gibberish that mocked his attempts to dial. He could feel the vibrations pounding in his chest, throbbing through the floor beneath his feet, echoing in every object inside the control room. "Close it – lower the shield!"

The bulky, gear-driven safeguard lethargically descended, locking into place to cover the observation window.

"It's getting louder. Is that the transducer, or something else?" Randy tried to answer his own question, scanning the instrument panels for signs of external interference. Information accumulated at an astounding rate, measurements fluctuated from moment to moment – nothing seemed constant, quantifiable or even reasonable. On the monitor, the dazzling light show continued with eruptions of colors that almost seemed rhythmic. Waves of heat leached through the steel-reinforced concrete walls. "Will that thing protect us?"

"I don't know – I hope so." A pulsating cadence emerged. Unlike the constant drone of the transducer, this sound clearly possessed a cyclic irregular pattern. "Christ, do you hear it? Do you feel it?"

"Like Morse code or something."

"Definitely of intelligent design – it must be."

The escalating resonance soon provided the researchers with a regrettable decision: Aborting the experiment prematurely would limit the amount of data available to analyze and might prevent them from being able to recreate the conditions; however, allowing the experiment to continue might well shake the old university science building to its foundations – destroying every shred of evidence the instruments had recorded and jeopardizing their lives.

"Abort on my word," Harley said. Randy dropped his pencil and paper and hunched over the keyboard. His fingers danced over the keys, inputting a series of commands. Harley winced and shook his head. It had gotten inside his head. The modulation invaded his skull, hammering the neurons in his brain. "This shouldn't be happening," he said, struggling not to lose consciousness. Harley forced his eyes wide in time to see Randy clawing at his own face. The monitor had gone black, but the lights had started seeping through the walls. "God, turn it off..."

3.

"Why is it so cold in here?" Tori Rogowicz had not gotten a full night's sleep all semester. With a full schedule of classes that kept her busy through lunchtime, and a tedious night job to keep her from starvation, she usually stayed up past midnight studying. "I'm gonna close the window, Claire – you don't mind, do you?"

"Nah, just let me sleep." Tori's roommate Claire managed to get a minimum of eight hours sleep every night – which generally meant she missed her first class of the morning. "I've got a give do a PowerPoint presentation in Yancey's class tomorrow."

Tori's eyes burned. She had been sitting in front of the computer for three hours working on a term paper for her Shakespeare class. Slowly, she pushed herself away from the desk and turned toward the window. She measured each step cautiously as her vision reacted to the change in vistas – the walls of the room blurred, the floor floated beneath her.

Most people never experience anything beyond that which lies immediately in front of them, blind to scenes and visions deliberately shrouded by dark designs or concealed in an elaborate disguise orchestrated by individual ignorance or fear.

Tori paused at the window, staring across the shadowed campus and into the night sky. The stars rippled as if someone had tossed a pebble into the twilight.

The weary student shrugged off the illusion, blaming it on fatigue and stress.

Some people recognize the existence of the unknowable, conceding that neither philosophy nor science can adequately explain away the mysteries of the cosmos. They sense the unseen horizons, the unobservable spectacle of worlds within worlds, the incalculable permutations of variant realities potentially coexisting alongside their palpable and perceivable environment.

Returning to her computer, Tori found the screen cluttered with gibberish – weird icons and symbols crawling across the monitor. Transfixed, she watched as incomprehensible shapes unfolded, multidimensional forms played out on the flat-screen monitor. The images stretched and distended, shifted and drifted, sprawled beyond the bounds that both logic and technology had fixed and seemed to reach out toward her.

"Shit!" Her big toe flipped the toggle switch on the power strip beneath the desk. "Son of a bitch!"

"What?" Claire poked her head out from beneath her pillow, sending the teddy bear her last boyfriend had given her tumbling to the floor. "What's the matter?"

"I think I got a virus, damn it." Tori gazed at the blackened screen still picturing the unrecognizable figures, too apprehensive to supply the power to reanimate it. "If my PC dies, I'm screwed."

"Don't worry about it – you've got antivirus software." Claire rolled over onto her stomach and yawned into her mattress. "You need some sleep. You're imaging things."

A few people experience moments of startling clarity, enlightening to some – terrifying to others. Theologians can cough up a number of terms to describe such an event: Nirvana, epiphany, spiritual transcendence. Such moments of complete illumination may result in innovation, inspiration or, on occasion, insanity.

Claire's voice only reached Tori as a muffled whisper. Still haunted by the things she had witnessed,

Tori now heard their audible signature – a deep, hypnotic resonance she could not escape.

The world's gentle façade melted away, leaving Tori unprepared to face its harsh, awful confessions.

4.

TAHLEQUAH, N.C. – An accident overnight claimed the life of one William Whitely student and critically injured another. Both students, working in the recently renovated Life Sciences building, were taken by ambulance to Tahlequah General Hospital around 1 a.m. following a 911 call from an unidentified source.

Randy Moody of Temple Terrace, Fla. was dead on arrival. Harley Saunders of Smithville, N.C. was listed in critical but stable condition. First responders, school officials and a hospital spokesperson would not discuss the circumstances of the accident pending notification of the victims' families.

From the *Haywood County Register*

5.

Ranier Nordhaus stood in the observation room surveying the damage. The fluorescent light overhead flickered and snapped though power to the whole building had been cut hours earlier. His cell phone vibrated eagerly in his pocket, its display glowing with bizarre digital representations the implications of which both intrigued and frightened him.

Outside, the city's fire marshal inspected the building for structural impairment. The team that responded to his call had been relieved shortly after dawn. Several complained of problems breathing, blurred vision and equilibrium issues. Nordhaus assured them that no radioactive materials had been used in the experiment, and that their sickness was likely related to "residual sonic reverberations" they had encountered during their search and rescue operations.

"There will be an inquiry, Ranier." College president Patricia Dempsey remained in the hallway outside the room. The door had been torn off its hinges during the rescue. It stood propped against the opposite wall of the corridor. Dempsey had come to the institution following some scandal at a New England private school, her position secured through means of connections and family wealth. She served William Whitely well, though, attracting a new circle of benefactors seemingly eager to contribute an endless flow of endowments. "It would be best if you considered stepping down, temporarily. I'll find an interim chairperson."

"I'm not stepping down," Nordhaus said, shuffling through notes Moody had scribbled on his legal pad. "You sent us down this path. I warned you there would be dangers."

"This is your department and your responsibility." Dempsey folded her arms across her chest, leaning forward to get a better view of the room. She recoiled when she spotted the pool of blood in the far corner of the room. "I gave you everything you needed to conduct your research."

"You gave me enough to buy the bare essentials. I only saw a fraction of those funds and you know it." Nordhaus leaned against the tabletop, felt it pulse beneath his touch. Though the transducer had been deactivated, something still resonated inside the laboratory. "The money you diverted from the grant would have bought us better safeguards against this kind of incident."

"Don't lecture me, Ranier," Dempsey glanced down the corridor, lowering her voice as a group of crime scene investigators approached. "There's plenty of blame to go around. We're both a party to this and we both want the same thing. I suggest we continue to work together to achieve it." She steadied herself, hands sweeping against her clothes brushing out unseen wrinkles compulsively. "We're in the same boat."

"We aren't in the same ocean," Ranier said, balking at the suggestion that he shared Dempsey's motivations. "My goal is to answer the mystery of existence through deliberate, calculated experimentation," he said. "Your goal is the accumulation of prestige and the accompanying prosperity."

"Shhhh..." The chief investigator thrust out a hand toward Dempsey and exhibited a suitable smile fitting the grim circumstances. "Patricia Dempsey," she said, "President of William Whitely."

Nordhaus paid no attention to the formalities and conversation that followed in the hallway as Dempsey vowed to extend every consideration to make those investigating the accident comfortable and well attended. She stopped short of barefaced bribery, but Nordhaus knew if she could find a way to circumvent the process through her acquaintances, she would not hesitate to do so.

Eventually, the investigators would want to see the laboratory. He would delay them if they requested access today, explaining that during the accident the existing safety measures had been activated and that access would not be possible for a full 24 hours. Technically, the justification was legitimate – but Nordhaus knew a way to get around it.

6.

Tori huddled in a corner of her room wrapped neatly in a quilt she purchased at an arts and crafts show in Gatlinburg several years earlier. She thought about the town on the other side of the Smoky Mountains, knew tourists would be lining up for miles in the coming weeks to see the leaves change. An annual pilgrimage for armchair naturalists, she had always been fascinated by the fall colors and their ability to draw such crowds.

Each year, spectators watched the world put on a different mask. Tori felt as though she had seen the world shed its skin that night, and she wrestled with the consequences.

Claire had reluctantly left for morning classes with a promise to return by noon to check roommate. She offered to fix her coffee before she left, but Tori refused. Her stomach had been in knots all night.

Though waves of nausea intermittently beleaguered her, her real concern was her vision.

The room floated, its vacillations vague but undeniable. Colors fluctuated wildly in bright light, pulsed visibly in the darkness. Tori saw things that could not be when she opened her eyes; when she closed them, the images did not always disappear. Her mind wrapped around solid objects to see them from all possible angles, curved around corners to reveal glimpses of things outside the scope of her vision.

She could see herself – not a reflection, but her true image as she sat cowering in her dorm room, her fingers gripping the fabric, her toes tucked beneath her feet inside her socks, her back pressed against the nightstand.

Before she left, Claire pulled the blinds down to keep the sun in check. She mentioned the activity across the campus lawn – fire trucks, ambulances and police cars gathered in front of the old Life Sciences building. Claire said the sound of sirens had interrupted her sleep. Tori did not remember hearing sirens. She heard something, though – something speaking to her in a language she could not understand. Something trying to communicate with her in a way that made her feel insignificant and primitive.

Something had gotten inside her head.

Her cell phone rang. Hesitantly, she slipped an arm out of her self-made cocoon and reached into her purse on the floor beside her bed. Thumbing the button, she pressed the phone to her hear.

"Hello," she said, but the word failed to take form. Instead, she grunted a monosyllabic groan.

"Tori?" Her mother called out across a cacophony of static and white noise, a dizzying dissonance of inexplicable interference that feigned intelligence. "Tori, can you hear me sweetie?"

Tori, her head swarming with blaring distractions, could no longer manage the faculty of speech. The slow, pitiful whimpers bubbling from her throat sounded childlike and slothful. Angrily, she threw the phone across the room. Even as it hit the floor, she felt it still resting in her hand, saw it still inside her purse, saw herself in an infinite number of different realities in a variety of familiar and unfamiliar situations. Time and space collapsed around her, smothering her with visions beyond her comprehension.

7.

TAHLEQUAH, N.C. – Another victim has been added to the recent wave of suicides at William Whitely College in the Blue Ridge Mountains near Asheville. April Bentley of Winston-Salem was found in her dorm room by a fellow student Thursday evening. County officials promised grieving parents they would investigate reports of a suicide pact among students.

A string of unfortunate events this fall has forced class cancellations, student relocations and a restructuring of the school's administration. The faculty shake-up included the termination of three board members who admitted accepting kickbacks from contractors renovating an unused campus building.

College president Patricia Dempsey condemned the actions of the board members and promised students and parents a speedy return to normalcy in the spring.

"I am certain William Whitely can overcome these tragedies," Dempsey said. "The school has brought in grief counselors and community monitors to help both students and staff cope with our recent losses. Classes will restart next week."

Bentley is the fifth student to commit suicide since mid-October. A memorial plaque for the first victim, Tori Rogowicz of Maggie Valley, will be unveiled on campus next week.
From the *Asheville Sun*

8.

Weeks after the accident, Nordhaus scanned the laboratory, the beam of his flashlight sweeping the debris. Ceiling tiles lay scattered on the floor. A few recognizable pieces of the transducer remained, though most of it had disintegrated into twisted metal, shattered circuit boards and fine powder. Overhead, structural supports had buckled. A single, concentrated burst of heat energy had melted paint off the walls, singed the floor tiles and warped the exposed corners of the blast shield.

With no lingering radiation, no traceable amounts of toxicity, he had agreed to grant investigators full access to the room the day after the incident. He did so with complete confidence they would find nothing they could understand. Ultimately, they relied upon his explanation.

Nordhaus had seen the tapes. He knew what happened. He also knew no one would believe him. Though the idea that parallel worlds exist had recently gained favor among theoretical physicists, even in principal the speculation sounded like pure science fiction. Nordhaus, along with at least a dozen other zealous disciples committed to proving the theory, considered our universe one bubble floating on an ocean of bubbles.

Unlike his peers, Nordhaus believed the best evidence to support the theory would come through physical contact with another universe. His studies, his hypotheses, his controversial research worked toward that end.

Now he had his proof – but he could not share it with the world for fear of the repercussions.

Nordhaus shined his flashlight on the invisible breach. He had discovered it accidentally, before the investigators had examined the room. His students, Saunders and Moody, had been on duty when the transducer – constantly varying its harmonic output – chanced on the frequency that opened a temporary portal between two or more parallel worlds. The result left one of them dead, the other mentally compromised.

The hell that had briefly manifested itself inside these four walls had dissipated – but its shadow remained.

As the beam swept the breach, light poured out of it from all angles, illuminating the entire room. Too infinitesimal to be seen, the rift still allowed particles of light to pass through from parallel worlds. Nordhaus knew light was not the only thing to exploit the minute portal.

"It went too far." Saunders startled Nordhaus. He shambled into the laboratory through the deserted observation room. He wore dark sunglasses, but his gaze remained fixed on the floor. He had lost weight and hair, and he looked pale and disheveled.

"Harley," Nordhaus reflexively directed the flashlight toward the student's face. "I didn't know you were still on campus. I thought you went home to spend a few months with your father."

"No. Doesn't matter where I go." He raised a hand to shield his eyes from the light. Nordhaus lowered the beam. "I'm tied to this, to this place."

"You just need to get some rest, Harley. You'll be alright."

"I don't know, Dr. Nordhaus." Saunders leaned against the wall. "I saw," he began, but lost the energy to put his memories into words. Nordhaus had met with him in the hospital during his recovery, had spoken with him on two other occasions since the accident. Saunders had been forthcoming with information about the night of the incident, and his testimony corroborated the data Nordhaus had managed to collect from the instruments in the observation room. "It's still here, isn't it?" Saunders glanced directly toward the breach. "I can see it."

"Yes," Nordhaus said. "It never sealed properly. Watch," he said, directing the flashlight beam toward it again. When the room flooded with radiance, Saunders trembled and turned away. Nordhaus turned off the light quickly. "Do you realize what's happening?"

Saunders, visibly shaken and anxious to leave the area, shook his head.

"At first, I thought that it was some kind of spatial anomaly – that the light from my flashlight was being refracted, scattered in different directions." Nordhaus grabbed Saunders by the shoulder, moved him closer to the door, positioning himself between the student and the breach. "Then I realized," he said, irresolute. His belief seemed so unconventional he had difficulty finding the words to explain it. "When I shine the light at the breach," Nordhaus said, "I am doing so in all the parallel worlds connected by it – only, in each one, I am standing at a slightly different spot in this room."

Saunders wept. He believed Nordhaus.

"Why didn't it close when the transducer stopped emitting?" Saunders threw his sunglasses to the floor, pressed the palms of his hands into his eyes. "Why can't I get it out of my head?"

Nordhaus guided Saunders out of the lab, through the observation room and into the corridor. Emergency lights painted small orbs on the tile in the hallway. A night watchman sat in a chair at the far end of the building reading the latest issue of *Hunter's World*.

"Light isn't the only thing that can pass through the portal; X-rays, radio waves – who knows what else. Since that night, people in the vicinity have reported all kinds of strange electronic abnormalities." Nordhaus dropped his gaze a little. "And, there are the suicides. I think some people were directly affected by energy discharged from the breach. It may have been accidental; it may have been intentional."

"What do you mean?"

"I think there have been attempts to communicate. Some people may have intercepted messages – encoded, electronic data our minds are not equipped to process."

"Nightmares?"

"Dreams, visions, hallucinations – the ones affected by it would probably be driven mad."

"I see them, Dr. Nordhaus. I see them when I sleep, I see them almost all the time." Saunders shivered, his tears repressed again. His eyes scanned empty space, tracing unseen figures and invisible forms. "Why won't they leave me alone?"

"Harley," Nordhaus said, noticing an occasionally flash of light emanating from the lab. In some alternate universe, he and Saunders were still inside. "I think the reason the portal didn't seal is because someone, or something, wants to keep it open. It may be me – a parallel version of me, anyway."

"Why?"

"I don't know. I only know that I see the danger now, and I am going to do what I can to stop it. Tomorrow, a crew will demolish half this building. They will fill that room with cement, make a tomb out of it. Lead shielding will encase it. Monitors will scan for any sign of activity, round the clock, for as long as I am employed by this college."

"What about the breach?"

"I can't close it," Nordhaus said. "But I'll slow down anything that tries to cross through it." Nordhaus saw the helplessness in his student's eyes, felt his fear and his uncertainty. In some parallel worlds, Moody had survived and Saunders had died when the portal opened. Nordhaus guessed that Saunders had come to that realization. "I could use some help." Saunders needed a purpose. "Someone with experience, someone who understands the need for confidentiality."

Saunders nodded, acknowledging both his understanding and acceptance. He left Nordhaus to collect the remaining equipment, to make a few final observations and prepare the area to be sealed forever in what he considered to be a high-tech sepulcher. Unlike Nordhaus, Saunders' accelerated perception had begun to untangle the labyrinth of possibilities, the countless deviations from their index world, concluding that while there were an infinite number of parallel worlds with insignificant differences, there also had to be an infinite number of parallel worlds with substantial aberrations.

From those worlds would come the horrors he had witnessed.

Saunders put his faith in Nordhaus and resigned himself to a lifetime of nightmares, teetering on the brink between omniscience and madness and waiting to see when something would penetrate the breach.

> "Once more unto the breach, dear friends, once more;
> Or close the wall up with our English dead!"
> Shakespeare, *King Henry V*, Act III, Scene I

What Sorrows May Come

1.

> **Yoder. Annie Mae,** daughter of Noah and Lydia Cripe, born near Smithville, North Carolina, Nov. 16, 1894; died at St. Mary's Teaching Hospital Nov. 1, 1934, of acute Bright's disease; aged 39. United in marriage to Amos Yoder June 17, 1917, in Arkham. Two sons and one daughter were born to this union. One son (Orvel Clinton) passed away Sept. 29, 1929. Formerly a member of Old Order Mennonite Church where she faithfully and willingly lived out its teaching. In Arkham, she attended the First Unitarian Church with her family. She leaves her deeply bereaved husband and two children (Simon and Mattie), and her parents. Funeral services Aug. 28 at First Unitarian. Burial in Chirstchurch Cemetery.

Amos held the paper in his trembling hands. He had read the clipping a hundred times through tearstained eyes – so many times the words echoed in his mind like a prayer committed to memory. Some nights, he still could not believe she had been taken from him.

Carefully, he folded the obituary and slipped it back between the pages of the Bible he kept in the bottom drawer of his nightstand – her family Bible. Its dog-eared, yellowed pages betrayed its great age. With margins embellished by notations his wife penned over the years in her mesmerizing handwriting, Amos more often read her comments and observations than he did the gospel. Scattered throughout the pages, he had also inserted her occasional love notes – mostly her starry-eyed responses to the letters he had written her in his youth during their courtship.

One particular letter he read often. She had penned it mere weeks before her death.

We are one; our souls merged in a union whose harmony makes the universe rife with envy. Nothing will sever the bond between us – not separation, not heartache and not death. Still, our fleeting immortality in this transitory corporeal existence eventually must render one of us temporarily unaccompanied. Do not for a moment believe that solitude should override reason and grant you sanction to seek a premature end. No matter what sorrows may come, what tragedies may afflict us we must always prevail and not yield to the enticement of relinquishing our responsibilities. Though it may be obscured by grief, there is always purpose.

Amos lay back against the pillow, allowing his gaze to drift out an open window and up into the starry skies overlooking the town of Arkham. He felt utterly detached from the universe, as remote as some distant, shunned world adrift in the darkness orbiting an extinguished star.

Regrets occupied these lonely hours, plaguing his conscience and depriving him of sleep. Had he not lost his teaching job at the college, he might have been able to afford better medical care for Annie Mae. Had he not been too proud to ask for financial help from her family, he might have been able to take her to see doctors in Boston. Had he not been so insistent upon working odd jobs at all hours of the night and day, he might have been more attentive to her needs, might have recognized the illness in her sooner, might have been able to do something.

Had he been a better man in some way, done something differently, Annie Mae might still be at his side – not resting in the bleak embrace of the cold and bitter earth in Christchurch Cemetery. Six months after her death, grief and guilt still suffocated him.

A knock at the door separated him from another unhealthy, self-induced immersion in remorse. Amos, in his night clothes and slippers, shambled across the floor, a blanket draped over his shoulders to shield him from the slight chill of the Arkham night. He cracked the door and peered out into the corridor.

"Sorry to disturb you at such a late hour, Mr. Yoder." Dr. Moamar Shalad, chairman of Miskatonic's Department of Oriental Studies, stood in the shadowed hallway of the apartment building. "I should have realized you would have retired for the evening," he paused, anxiously scanning the hallway with darting eyes. "It's just – I was working late in the library, and I have some concerns."

"Concerns?"

"Corrections, I should say." Shalad worked long hours taking every advantage of his appointment at Miskatonic, burying himself in ancient tomes, scrutinizing texts to produce accurate translations, gleaning shards of forgotten knowledge from complex and esoteric medieval occult treatises. "Corrections to my manuscript. Very important corrections I must convey at your earliest convenience."

"It will have to wait until morning," Amos said, resting his head against the door. "I won't have access to the material until then."

"Yes, morning is good." Shalad spoke with a British accent, punctuated with Arabic inflections. Mild-mannered and somewhat reclusive, Shalad slowly backed away from the doorway, bowing in unnecessary gratitude. His eyes still swept the darkness surrounding him, his head jerking unnaturally to accommodate his restlessly drifting gaze. "I will see you in the morning. And please," he added, clasping his hands as if preparing to plead, "Please – no more editing until I can indicate the changes to be made, yes? Yes, alright. Thank you."

Amos nodded and closed the door.

Shalad often came across as eccentric and compulsive but Amos had learned to appreciate his neighbor's unconventional idiosyncrasies. He was, in fact, friendlier than any of the other tenants in the residence.

With Simon away at school, and Mattie living with her grandparents in Smithville, Amos decided to rent out the two-story house on East Church St. where he and Annie Mae had raised the children. He collected his most treasured belongings, condensed them into a few boxes and packed everything else into the attic for safekeeping. He took a vacancy at the Guardian Apartments, a three-room apartment with various amenities including an icebox and a gas stove.

The financial woes of the nation had begun to fade, and jobs had become more plentiful in Arkham. Amos found steady work in a job which fit his professional credentials. Before the depression forced the college to thin its faculty, he had taught undergraduate composition as an adjunct at Miskatonic. Still waiting for a new teaching position to open, Amos ran into Malcolm Bunden of Bunden's Bindery who immediately offered him a salaried position as senior proofreader and copy editor.

Shalad's upcoming thesis currently demanded his attentions. Bunden had warned Amos that Shalad would pester him incessantly, constantly seeking to revise his work, adding passages, deleting references, expanding some sections while eliminating others. He had developed an infamous reputation at the bindery – a nitpicker, a dithering scholar, a man obsessed with precision working in a field filled with ambiguities and uncertainties.

Amos settled back into bed, shrugging off the intrusion and eventually yielding to sleep.

In the hours prior to dawn, his dreams afforded him neither comfort nor sanctuary. He dreamed of Annie Mae, alone and barefooted beneath a slivered moon stained crimson red. She shuffled aimlessly across a weedy meadow peppered with shrunken, wasted flowers and grim, gray headstones.

He swayed beneath a sycamore towering over the center of the glade, arms stretching towards her in an inconsolable embrace. His attempts to call to her failed – no matter how he tried, he could find no voice.

As he watched helplessly, the ground beneath her liquefied. Slowly, the earth swallowed her.

2.

Residents of Arkham first noticed the Stranger in early November, after the leaves had passed the peak of their annual spectacle and had been collected in compost heaps on the manicured lawns of residents. Seen only in the final hour before nightfall as the sun slipped from the colorless skies in its daily abandonment of the city to the absolutism of twilight and the apathetic moon, he materialized most often along the narrow streets of the French Hill district. His fascination with certain edifices – particularly the wretchedly neglected and boarded-up Bayfriar's Church and the ill-famed rooming house at 197 East Pickman Street – caused local denizens to abandon their custom of relaxing on front porches in the evening and discussing the days events.

"You have seen him then?" Dr. Cameron, Dean of the School of Physical Sciences spoke softly, cautiously. He sat across from Dr. Upham, chair of Miskatonic's Department of Mathematics and Dr. Shalad in a conference room in Locksley Hall. "The similarity is certainly striking."

"I knew him well," Upham said, nervously nibbling on a pencil. "Well enough to recognize him even now, years later. But in the state he is in, it is hard to say." The Stranger bared an uncanny resemblance to a former mathematics student from Haverhill. Described by his mentors as a genius, the undergraduate had become so obsessed with the complexities of quantum physics and non-Euclidian geometry that he lost all perception of reality. His descent into madness and his subsequent disappearance still troubled his counselors at the college, and his fate remained something of a mystery. "This Stranger – if it is him – why would he not approach us? Why has he returned?"

"Llanfer swears he's been in the library after hours." Cameron sipped his tea gracefully, a model of New England etiquette. "Perhaps you've seen him there during your studies, Dr. Shalad."

"No," Shalad answered quickly. Though always quiet, his reticence at the table during the current conversation far surpassed his usual reluctance to engage in dialogue. "I've not seen him."

"Surely, you've heard others mention him," Upham said, raising an eyebrow. "The Stranger – that's what the locals call him – has been turning up all over Arkham."

Shalad shook his head and frowned. He stared at his hands, hoping the others would not recognize the indignity in his eyes.

"It is his awful appearance that has people gossiping." Cameron slanted forward over the table. "Short, dirty and unkempt. Face unshaven and unclean, with wild eyes and an angry scowl. Pale and emaciated. Clothes grubby, trousers tattered at the cuff, shirt untucked and soiled with sweat and dirt." Cameron eased back into his chair, an uneasy smile blossoming on his face. "Hardly the student I remember. It must be nothing more than coincidence."

"I hope you are right," Upham said.

"I hope you'll excuse me, gentlemen," Shalad said abruptly, "I have forgotten an appointment this morning regarding my manuscript." Shalad hastily gathered his belongings and left the room without further explanation, leaving Cameron and Upham staring after him with puzzled expressions.

3.

Shalad's manuscript had taken up residence in a corner of Amos Yoder's desk several weeks earlier. Like a mule-headed squatter, much of it loitered in the same untidy heap it had assumed upon its arrival, feigning indifference but secretly begging for attention. Amos loathed proofing translations – particularly those whose subject matter dated to times of antiquity. Still, he had found Shalad's work meticulous and accurate, and expected to find few errors to mark for correction.

"Sorry I am late," Shalad said, startling Amos as he approached his office unannounced. The proofreader's desk faced a drab, dull and windowless wall in a remote and quiet niche in bindery's basement. Aside from the desk and an uncomfortable chair, the only other piece of furniture the bindery could afford to offer Amos was a water-damaged, old bookcase which housed a variety of reference books. Shalad lingered in the doorway, unable to find a comfortable place to stand in the room. "It is almost noon – I was distracted by a student's inquiry during a morning class and..."

"No need for apologies, Dr. Shalad." Amos patted Shalad's manuscript. "I've been busying myself with other projects, smaller in scope. I've only read about a quarter of your work."

"Oh, my," Shalad said, looking somewhat troubled, "That much already you have seen?"

"Roughly. And may I congratulate you on your attention to detail." Amos picked up a stack of typewritten pages he had already reviewed, leafing through them proudly. "No significant mistakes, no typographical errors – only a handful of my marks, mostly indicating spacing issues for the typesetters."

"Thank you, thank you," Shalad nodded courteously, but the concern lingered in his expression and in his voice. His eyes began darting around in their sockets again, his head twitched noticeably from side to side as if he expected to catch sight of something in his peripheral vision. "Have you," he said after an extended and unnerving pause, "Have you gotten to the section on 12th century necromantic philosophy?"

"No," Amos answered abruptly, hoping to relieve Shalad of his unspecified distress. "In fact, I think I left off just before your introduction to that portion of the text."

"That is exceptionally good news," Shalad cracked a nervous smile and scratched the dark whiskers of his beard. His apprehension shrank but did not entirely evaporate as Amos had hoped. His persistent trepidation made Amos increasingly tense, as if his unexplained fear had become contagious. "I am afraid that upon reflection, I must make extensive revisions," he said repentantly, lowering his voice. In a whisper, he continued, "Mistakes were made. Most terrible mistakes."

"I doubt that," Amos said, though the solemnity with which Shalad had made his confession disconcerted him. "Your thoroughness is legendary. I'm sure whatever your oversights might be, they are more trivial than you believe."

"I only wish that were the case, dear friend." Shalad faltered, shivering as if touched by an icy hand. "My omissions are indeed dire, and have put at risk my career and my life alike." The professor began swaying from side to side, struggling to keep his balance and his consciousness. "I only hope I can make the necessary revisions before it is too late."

His cryptic revelation still floating in the cool air of the bindery basement, Shalad's apparent exhaustion and anxiety caught up with him in a moment of unguarded frailty. He suddenly slumped forward, eyes rolling back into his head as he collapsed in the doorway.

"Dr. Shalad? Moamar?" Amos caught the professor's wiry frame and lowered him to the floor carefully.

Amos started to call for help, to summon Malcolm Bunden whose own office was one floor up, its door always open. Something held his tongue – something instinctive prompted him to manage the situation single-handedly, without making a spectacle of it. Perhaps he did so out of empathy, appreciating Shalad's private nature and recognizing the event as a potential source of social embarrassment for him. Then again, perhaps Shalad's own fear unconsciously motivated him not to call attention to the man's momentary debility.

Retrieving a bottle of smelling salts from his desk drawer, Amos roused Shalad from the fringes of oblivion.

"What," Shalad shuddered, his eyelids tentatively lifting. His face contorted with short-lived horror as though he faced a vision of his own death at the very moment of his awakening. Mumbling, he continued, rather cryptically, "This is not the time. We must consult in private."

"There's no one else here, Moamar." Amos knelt beside the professor, waiting for him to regain his composure and fix his shifting gaze. His assurance seemed of little impact, and he wondered for a moment if Shalad had been addressing him or some other imagined – or invisible – entity. Nonetheless, he repeated assertion and reminded his friend of his whereabouts. "We're in my office at the bindery. We're completely alone."

"Yes," Shalad said, "Yes, I remember." With his wits returning, Shalad's face grew flush with humiliation. "Mr. Yoder, forgive my infirmity. I have not been myself these last few weeks, suffering from spells and seizures." His admission dredged up memories of Annie Mae's last weeks. Before the malady claimed her, it plagued her with fainting spells and frightening convulsions. Amos had been forced to watch as her precious life withered, her vitality waned, her beauty and charm shriveled under the burden encumbrance of disease. "I should rest more, but there is much more work to be done."

"You can not accomplish your work if you are not fit," Amos said.

"Perhaps." Shalad awkwardly returned to his feet. "I will rest this afternoon. Would it be possible to delay our meeting until this evening?"

"I think it would be to your benefit."

"Agreed." Shalad eyed the manuscript on the desk. "I would like to take the section of my manuscript that is to be corrected."

"It is your manuscript," Amos said, smiling. He picked up the pages the professor had requested and handed them to him. "But I would hope you would spend more time relaxing than revising this afternoon."

"Your advice is well received, Mr. Yoder." Shalad carefully tucked the pages beneath his arm, holding them close against his chest. "This evening then, shortly after dinner?"

"Very well."

4.

The Stranger waited patiently inside the abandoned house of worship on East Church Street, the dimming light of day shining through gaps in the boards covering the windows. The place reeked of rats' nests and pigeon waste. The shadows swarmed with insects as the wind howled around the soot-tinged steeple creating a wailing whisper that filled the air with tangible melancholy.

Dr. Shalad gained access to Bayfriar's church through a forgotten doorway almost wholly concealed by thick vines.

"Have you brought it?"

"I have not," Shalad answered nervously. The Stranger realigned himself in the light revealing the pallid, lesion-covered flesh of his awful face and eyes half submerged in their sockets. "I will bring you the new translation tonight, after midnight." Shalad winced at the stench of death. Beneath the Stranger's tattered, rotting flesh, worms yet toiled devouring the remnants of his mortal coil. "You must wait here. Too many have seen you, you risk discovery."

"I have nothing left to risk," the Stranger said, scarcely concealing his aggravation. The madness and obsession he had wrestled with in life continued to plague him in death, and Shalad suspected he had wrought dark designs in his seclusion, planning to use his genius to assemble legions of hideous allies from unimagined worlds. "I will wait, because I can no longer summon the strength to do what must be done." He faltered a little, recoiling back into the shadows. His power waned, and Shalad could sense his growing infirmity. "Don't think I cannot carry out my threats against you, Shalad," he warned, authority returning to his voice. "You are responsible for this, and you will see to it that my reanimation is complete so that I may complete my work."

Shalad nodded in silent understanding. He vowed to finish the job before dawn stirred legend-haunted Arkham.

5.

Shalad failed to appear for some time after dinner. As the evening progressed, Amos visited his apartment several times. Each time he knocked on Shalad's door, he thought he heard sounds coming from inside, but the professor did not respond. He hoped Shalad had taken his recommendation and had spent the afternoon away from his studies.

Shortly after midnight, Amos felt safe in assuming Dr. Shalad had forgotten their appointment. He turned off all the lights in the apartment, cracked his bedroom window, sat on the edge of his bed and reread Annie Mae's obituary – a ritual he carried out nightly.

On the nightstand, a straight razor waited quietly. It kept its thirst discreetly censored, stifling the urge to glimmer in the moonlight. It made no perceptible promises, offered no guarantees of being able to end suffering. Silence and persistence served as deadlier enticements to a man like Amos. For six months, he had let the blade remain at his bedside, collecting dust. He still needed the comfort of an accessible, dependable escape should his grief prove too much to bear.

On more than one occasion, the razor had found its way into his hands. Each time, he found some reason to put it aside again.

Amos managed a noble charade in public, always acting properly and politely around Malcolm Bunden and the bindery's clients; attending church services regularly; corresponding with his children and Annie Mae's relatives. He lived from day to day, surviving on the bare necessities, feigning interest in his work, his acquaintances and his future.

In fact, his life had become hollow – a black void opened up at the heart of him the day he lost Annie Mae, and it grew larger each day. He rotted from the inside without the cold comfort of death. Without her, existence was meaningless. His children – both on the verge of adulthood – would be cared for by their grandparents and would, ultimately, be better off without the burden of having to watch a sad widower squander away his remaining years in misery and seclusion.

Amos felt his fingers caressing the razor, his warm touch contrasting with its icy proposition.

He placed the news clipping back into the Bible, set the Bible in the drawer and closed it.

He examined his wrist, the serpentine blue vein beneath the delicate veil of flesh. He considered that at his funeral, they would have to pull his sleeves low to conceal the scars – then realized his palms would be faced down, his arms folded over his stomach in a simulation of tranquility and dignity.

Death had no dignity, neither for the living or the dead. Amos no longer knew whether to believe in paradise, purgatory or oblivion. Whatever waited on the other side of the barrier, it had to be better than the inane anguish of his inconsequential life.

He pressed the blade gently against his skin, depressing it until a tiny bead of blood appeared. Amos closed his eyes, took the absence of pain as an omen.

Had the pounding at the door come a moment later, it would have been too late. Pulled back from the edge by fickle fate, Amos placed the razor back on the edge of the nightstand, tugged on the sleeve of his nightshirt and matted the smear of blood staining his wrist.

"My apologies again, Mr. Yoder," Shalad stood several paces from the door, enveloped in inky darkness. "I was kept from our meeting by circumstances beyond my control. My concern for your safety, however, necessitated this late visit." The professor leaned into the light spilling from the apartment. His eyes wide and teeming with angst, he clutched Amos' left arm and turned it upright, exposing the wound which continued to weep droplets of blood. "She told me to stop you," he said, "She told me to tell you that no matter what sorrows may come, what tragedies may afflict you; you must always prevail and not yield to the enticement of relinquishing your responsibilities."

Amos recognized the words immediately – though how they could have been uttered with such precision by

Shalad he could not guess. As Amos wavered in disbelief, Shalad shot impatient glances down the corridor, unmistakably expecting to see someone – or something. After a few moments, he pushed Amos back into the apartment and followed, closing the door behind him.

"She told me you had come to this," Shalad said, grabbing Amos's arm.

"Annie Mae?" Amos followed Shalad's gaze down to his wrist. The telltale incision joined a dozen others that had not healed, each a reminder of how tenuous the barrier between life and death had become for Amos. "How?"

"Necromancy, of course." Shalad relinquished his grasp, and Amos' arm fell to his side. "The process is academic. It is the interpretation that challenges the novice and adept alike."

"You spoke with her?" Amos knew enough about the medieval divinatory practice Shalad and other Miskatonic scholars had examined in their writings, but he never knew them to admit to conducting such ceremonial rites. "You spoke with Annie Mae?"

"Yes, for some time this evening." Shalad's response came in a blunt tone that irritated Amos, filling him with both jealousy and distrust. "Well," he continued, "She spoke to me through myriad voices, entities which have helped me sort out certain discrepancies in my theories. Their guidance will allow me to revise my manuscript and rectify a situation my ignorance and zeal brought about."

"I don't understand."

"Nor could you, Mr. Yoder." Shalad gripped Amos' shoulder, realizing his sudden revelations must have sounded like utter madness. "You would not believe me if I told you that, given the proper variables, I could sketch a doorway with charcoal or some other writing implement, and cause it to become real simply by its design." Shalad scanned Amos' eyes, searching for a glimmer. He hoped not for comprehension but for an inkling of faith. "If I suggested that I could pass through a mirror into another world, you would surely see me committed to an asylum.

And yet, the phenomenon is real, possessing a complex but rational scientific explanation.

"There are passages all around us, some occurring naturally, some created long ago and long ago abandoned. These conduits, used properly, can be used to communicate with entities that have passed beyond the mortal sphere and into other dimensions." He recalled with pride his first successful experiment, piercing the barrier separating dimensions. "At first, I thought I was speaking directly with the deceased. I made contact with relatives and friends, asked questions only they could answer. But I found they also answered questions they could not answer – possessed knowledge they should not possess. It was as if I was conversing with an amalgamation of higher beings, some part of which formerly comprised individuals I knew."

"And that is why you must revise your manuscript."

"If only that proved to be my gravest mistake." Shalad shuddered, recalling the terrible Stranger awaiting him in Bayfriar's Church. "My initial attempts led to an unfortunate consequence and unanticipated discovery – the channels by which communication is made possible may also be used to redistribute the energy of a life force. I unintentionally allowed such an essence to travel back to this world, to reanimate its former shell – and tonight, I must destroy it, once and for all."

6.

Against Dr. Moamar Shalad's implicit instructions, Amos Yoder felt compelled to forsake the moderate safety of his residence at the Guardian Apartments, cross the Miskatonic and take to the narrow, shadowed avenues of French Hill beneath the gloaming. Arkham had a reputation for being two different cities occupying the same patch of land in the valley. By day, Arkham exhibited a distinctly patrician air denoting its proud scholarly institution and the principled decorum and respectability of its denizens. The moon displaced the dignified face of the city, kindling its cryptic secrets, highlighting its most disreputable neighborhoods and dredging up its most notorious scandals and the many disgraces tarnishing its history.

Bayfriar's Church towered over the surrounding neighborhoods, maligned with neglect and haunted by some whispered wickedness of old. A shrine to all things secreted in Arkham, its boarded windows and padlocked doors fell far short of hiding its shame – particularly when the knowing twilight assessed its merits.

Amos found Shalad outside the old church, half-crouching in the weeds.

"He's taken it – he's taken the manuscript," Shalad said, coughing for air. "He had more strength than I thought."

"Who?" Amos helped Shalad to his feet.

"I will not speak his name – it might serve to increase his power." Shalad, in poor health and weakened further by exhaustion, struggled to stand. "He must not be allowed to complete the transference. He will become too dangerous."

"What can I do?"

"Go to the cemetery – follow him, to Christchurch," Shalad said. Amos now noticed the blood and bruises covering his face. The Stranger had taken advantage of Shalad, convinced him of his frailty lulling him into false confidence. "The portal remains open – go and call her, she will do what must be done."

Amos traced the winding path of Powder Mill Street, where decaying houses dating to the late 18th century leaned into the lane. Overcrowded and populated by the impoverished, the neighborhood boasted bloated shadows in blind alleys, malodorous filth in inadequate sewers and the constant impression of ongoing veiled perversions in dingy, crumbling dwellings.

With every step, Amos felt as if the night air had been tinged with the passing of something awful, something menacing and incongruous – a degenerate pariah with appalling aspirations.

When he reached Christchurch Cemetery, an eerie green glow drew him to its center where the old sycamore stretched its weary arms as if it alone supported the starry canopy of the night sky. The Stranger, on his knees, worked frantically under the glow of some unearthly radiance – perhaps the glow of souls enslaved. A twisted branch clenched by his flesh-ragged fist, he scrawled unfamiliar symbols into the damp clay of the graveyard representing forgotten formulae. His etchings resembled mathematician's chalkboard more than a medieval wizard's mystic renderings.

Amos pressed himself against a nearby headstone, shielding himself from discovery amidst charnel shadows.

"All those secrets kept from me," the Stranger said, muttering to himself, "Now will be revealed."

The cemetery floor trembled with agitation and apprehension as if the dead writhed in their coffins. Amos felt it in his bones, the stirring of ancient things long banished, the barriers breaking down around him. Had he glanced overhead, he would have trembled as the stars, one by one, began to desert the sky. Instead, his gaze chanced downward, his eyes suddenly fixed to the inscription upon the stone sheltering him.

"Annie Mae," he said softly, as all the grief and sorrow in the world fell upon him.

Thunder immediately followed the flash of lightning as it struck the old sycamore, flooding the cemetery with blinding light. Flames sprouted from its uppermost limbs, dancing on the tips of wilting twigs and spreading from limb to limb. The fire ebbed promptly, though, as rain erupted from the cloudless sky.

The Stranger had been thrown to the ground and scrambled to complete his task. His labors proved futile as the downpour washed away all his efforts.

Amos watched from the distance, his chin resting on the headstone as tears sprang to his eyes. His anguish dissipated as he felt a gentle hand rest upon his shoulder.

"Whatever sorrows may come," Annie Mae said, whispering into his ear, "Be strong for me. There is always purpose. We will be reunited when the time comes."

Amos turned, hoping to see her face, hoping to look into her eyes one more time. He found nothing but empty air beside him. On the outskirts of the cemetery, he saw a shambling figure – Dr. Shalad had finally caught up with him.

Turning back toward the sycamore, Amos watched as a brightly lit entity appeared, towering over the weeping Stranger. The ground beneath them seemed to liquefy, and in an instant, the earth swallowed them both.

Their Prison Ordained in Utter Darkness

1.
[Sept. 11, 1958 – Five Spot Café, New York City]

    Carter Hexam had been nursing a beer for more than an hour before he noticed his contact dawdling near the hatcheck booth, then, gradually, weaving his way through the vestibule toward the smoke-filled main hall.
    A sizeable joint compared to many New York City jazz clubs, the Five Spot Café attracted a standing-room-only crowd that evening, those in the know eagerly anticipating a rumored reunion. Hexam hoped to conduct his official business speedily so he could savor the music.
    Situated on Cooper Square on the outskirts of the Bowery neighborhood, the Five Spot Café had become something of a mecca for musicians, artists and writers. The bar – tended this evening by brothers Joe and Iggy, owners of the establishment – ran the length of one wall. The remaining walls had been plastered with posters and flyers promoting jazz concerts, artist exhibits and gallery openings.
    "Evening, Carter," Oscar Pendleton said, collapsing into the chair opposite Hexam. He looked tired, spent. More than 20 years older than Hexam, Pendleton was short and stocky, red-faced and predominantly bald. "Place is packed tonight, huh?"
    "Yes sir." In contrast to Pendleton, 36-year-old Hexam was tall and lean, wiry but reasonably muscular, with the sinewy physique of a marathoner. Clean-shaven, he had iron gray hair and piercing blue eyes. "Monk's playing. Word has it Coltrane is sitting in for Johnny Griffin."
    "That would explain it." Pendleton quietly surveyed the shadow-haunted jazz club, scanning the audience looking for potential adversaries. His reflexive diligence

betrayed old habits – the place probably evoked memories of decadent Berlin cabarets during the Weimar Republic era. "Not my cup of tea," Pendleton said. "I prefer Bach, Beethoven, you know."

"You sound like my father."

"He was a good man," Pendleton said, speaking with a serene sincerity. A brief moment of silence ensued, interrupted by a jazz aficionado looking to share a table. The gangly young fellow wearing a navy-blue turtle-neck sweater and khaki corduroy trousers shuffled a bit too close to the table and got a menacing grimace from Pendleton. The implicit warning sent the youth off in another direction. "Still miss him. I know you do, too."

"We both knew the risks," Hexam said coldly. He would not allow himself the liability of lingering grief. His father died in the line of service, a noble death. His commitment to the greater good distinguished him as a hero to his family ... and in Hexam's family, for three generations running, the struggle to manage malevolence and counterbalance catastrophic hazards took precedence over all else. "I believe you have something for me?"

"Indeed." Pendleton placed a dossier on the table, tapping it three times. The number of taps indicated the level of urgency: Three taps meant the assignment objective was pressing but not critical – a subtle distinction, but one that assured Hexam that doomsday was not at hand. "This is the vacation packet you requested. Five brochures, total," he said, revealing that his overseers anticipated the mission would place him in as many as five foreign countries. "Fascinating itinerary. Wish I was in better shape."

Pendleton, Hexam's current Task Handler, had seen better days. He had become a paper-pusher, a glorified courier with an official-sounding title. The Office of Strategic Preservation – the agency employing both men – venerated him for his war-time exploits in Europe, battling ritualistic mystics that formed the core of Himmler's rabid Ahnenerbe offshoot. The injuries he had sustained in action, however, would keep him from ever returning to active duty.

"And just to be clear, don't take any rickshaws," Pendleton added, asserting that the OSP would not take kindly to any unauthorized forays behind the Bamboo Curtain. "It's all in the packet, though. Read through the material carefully, especially the fine print."

"Of course. Do I have a departure date?"

"Day after tomorrow." A waiter wearing a tidy red jacket, slightly oversized, detoured through the crowd when he noticed the new arrival, but Pendleton snubbed him. He had no intention of staying any longer than necessary. "That will give you some time to break the news to the wife and kids."

"I appreciate that."

"How is Sharon?"

"Fine, fine."

"And the children?"

"Splendid," Hexam said. He generally avoided discussing his family with coworkers, but, sensing Pendleton's curiosity had not yet been satisfied, he continued. "The twins just started school. Marlene has decided she wants to be a poet and Amber is still pursuing her dream of becoming Broadway's next ingénue."

"Good," Pendleton said, his gaze drifting around the room. Joe was lining up glasses of beer along the bar for the waiter while Iggy helped escort an empty-pocketed skid-row drunkard out onto the front sidewalk. "Guess I'll call it a night, then."

"Good seeing you," Hexam said, trying to sound pleasant. "I'll look this over. If I have any questions – "

"If you have any questions, contact me through the normal channels and we'll set up a meeting." Pendleton stood, groaning a little as his body resisted a shift from inertia. "Take care of yourself."

Hexam ordered another beer and the night bore down on him from all sides. Smoke, droning chatter and shadows converged creating a static euphoria. He perused the bogus travel brochures as Roland Hanna played an hour-long set, deciphering what he could. The "fine print" Pendleton had mentioned alluded to data stored in microdots, accessible only with the use of a microscope.

Less sensitive data had been encrypted in the seemingly banal content of the professional-grade leaflets.

His mission, he gathered, would send him to Southeast Asia, with his primary objective being a rendezvous on the island of Quemoy off the coast of the Chinese mainland. Other potential theaters included Japan, Laos, Thailand and Burma, home of the notorious Tcho-Tcho people. Hexam suppressed an impulsive shudder at the thought of them. He hoped his undertaking would not bring him into their sphere of influence.

For now, the details of his assignment would have to wait.

Thelonious Monk arrived late, charging straight through the main room as the fervent crowd parted with Biblical precision. Monk wore his signature tweed hat, heavy tan jacket and a dark, thin necktie. He disappeared into the kitchen, making his way to the dressing room. Within a few minutes, the quartet was filing out of the back and making its way onto the bandstand: First, Monk took his place in front of the piano, quickly followed by bassist Ahmed Abdul-Malik and drummer Roy Haynes.

The rumors proved accurate: Tenor saxophonist John Coltrane emerged from the shadows and a buzz surged through the crowd.

The quartet slid gently into the sparse yet evocative "Crepuscule with Nellie," Monk attacking the ivory with meticulous fanaticism. He played the song he had written for his wife with keen and genuine emotion, and the crowd, brimming with voyeuristic glee, listened intently to the musical love note.

Quickly, the quartet shifted into a 10-minute rendition of "Trinkle Tinkle," an eccentric and dynamic number showcasing Coltrane's fluid solos. The accomplished musician, swinging from one tone to another, reveled in his own brand of harmonic havoc. Monk's own minimalism grounded the piece, hefty chords and flowing phrasing contrasting Coltrane's frenzied strolling.

At a nearby table, a patron – engrossed in the music – inadvertently displaced his drink, sending it crashing to the floor. The tumult of breaking glass led to short-lived bedlam: gasps, giggles and incoherent gibbering spread like ripples from the epicenter. Coltrane cleverly echoed the flash of madness with a fleeting staccato extemporization, his own on-the-spot invention mirroring a moment of chaos.

Chaos.

Bebop relied upon disorder and improvisation. It demanded a certain degree of creative mayhem. Avant-garde jazzmen like Coltrane and Monk played along the periphery of pandemonium, courting chaos unabashedly. To Hexam, filaments of chaos could be found everywhere: in music, in traffic patterns, in history books and certainly in the perplexities of world events.

Given the choice between order and chaos, the cosmos always migrated towards anarchy. At its core, the universe preferred turmoil and, over hundreds of billons of years, it would succeed in achieving it at the expense of whatever far-flung civilizations survived that far into the future.

Of course, Hexam also knew that certain entities – given the opportunity – would blissfully accelerate the process.

2.
[Sept. 17, 1958 – Tokyo]

The overnight layover in Tokyo, Japan, pleased Carter Hexam: The respite would allow him the opportunity to quiz an old acquaintance about relevant subject matter.

Before departing from New York, Hexam arranged for transportation and lodging and – upon arrival – quickly found his driver. Squeezing into a diminutive Renault Floride, Hexam provided directions to a quaint Japanese inn on the Sumida River near the Shimbashi Bridge. The car sped off into the twilight.

An hour later, having traversed every conceivable darkened side-street in the city, the car came to rest beneath a streetlamp on a narrow lane. The traditional inn boasted an attractive pagoda-form entrance and picturesque garden filled with dwarf shrubbery.

Instead of the customary welcome from the inn's proprietors – usually dressed in traditional garments and frozen in the most gracious pose conceivable in anticipation of a new lodger – Hexam found himself approaching a tall, dour middle-aged American puffing placidly on a Cuban cigar.

"What have you gotten yourself into this time, Hexam?"

"I was hoping you could help me sort that out, seeing as you know everything that happens in this hemisphere." Hexam extended his hand, renewing an old friendship. "How long has it been since we crossed paths, Frank?"

"A good five years, I'd guess." Frank Barlow, formerly with the American military, had so enjoyed his tour of duty during the postwar occupation of Japan that he decided to stay. Although retired, he continued to provide intelligence to various branches of the American government as necessity required. "I hear they have you chasing flying saucers these days."

"Not exactly," Hexam said, slightly aggrieved by the insinuation. Barlow – a man of considerable knowledge and experience – knew perfectly well that the Office of Strategic Preservation had little to do with the disinformation being parceled out by other government agencies to mislead the public. "But that can wait. I'm hungry."

After depositing Hexam's luggage at the inn, the two strolled to a nearby restaurant. In between gulps of saké, Hexam and Barlow enjoyed eel soup and a variety of seafood offerings, each beguilingly exhibited as miniature masterpieces upon the plate with meticulous care. Each dish displayed exquisite attention to color, texture, detail and order.

Order.

The Japanese had a knack for creating harmony out of turmoil, even in nature.

"So, what relic has the OSP so excited they're willing to send one of their best assets into a war zone?" Though Barlow did not have adequate clearance to learn the true purpose of the Office of Strategic Preservation, he had ascertained enough details over the years to develop practical speculation. His conjecture often manifested itself in subtle quips. "Must be something unique – out of this world, even."

"Would you happen to be familiar with an archeologist named Tsum Um Nui?"

"No," Barlow said gruffly, leaning back in his chair. "In fact, that's not even a proper name – not in Chinese or Japanese." He paused, gauging his friend's reaction. "Don't look so glum, chum. So happens I know who you're talking about anyway."

"But how could you – "

"Old Tsum Um Nui has popped up in a dozen communiqués over the last few years regarding some research supposedly done back in the late 1930s in China and Tibet," Barlow explained. "The name is plain subterfuge; whoever this fellow was, he's long dead now. The Soviets have taken a particular interest in digging up information about him."

"What about his research?"

"Hokum, according to any academicians you question," Barlow said. "Some nonsense about stone discs and spaceship that crashed in the mountains thousands of years ago."

Barlow's description matched the OSP's data: Intelligence gatherers in Formosa claimed the defector possessed a 12,000-year-old jade disc forged by beings not of this world.

"So there's nothing to it?"

"Well, that depends on who you ask." Barlow eyeballed the restaurant and, finding it mostly cleared of late-night clientele, continued. "Should you ask a member of the Tong of the Silver Shadow, you might get a completely different story. Unfortunately, they would also probably kill you and eat your face – not necessarily in that order."

"Charming," Hexam said, sipping saké. "Sounds a bit too much like the Tcho-Tcho people."

"Yes, kissing cousins, I'm sure," Barlow said. "Anyway, the Silver Shadow thugs would tell you that the discs are actually keys to hidden gateways scattered all over place."

"Gateways to what?"

"You're the OSP agent, man," Barlow said. "Have you ever heard of a hidden gateway that led some place you wanted to go for a holiday? It's Hell, the Inferno, the Abyss, the Infinite Gulf of Darkness – doesn't matter what name you assign it, it's the source of every nightmare visited upon mankind."

"Right." The pieces had begun falling into place for Hexam. The Office of Strategic Preservation had already managed to map out a number of extra-dimensional portals strewn across the planet – doorways designed by highly advanced engineers millions of years ago. Many led to parallel worlds and distant galaxies. Many contained hostile entities – ancient horrors long imprisoned, waiting impatiently for liberation. "I can see how such an artifact could be dangerous if it fell into the wrong hands."

"Do you have smog in the noggin, Hexam?" Barlow shook his head, shocked his old friend had become subservient to an ideology. "Such an artifact would be dangerous *in anyone's hands*. The OSP isn't the pinnacle of righteousness."

"True enough," Hexam admitted. "But I'll clue you in on one thing, Frank: It's far less malevolent than the alternative right now. One way or another, the relic will come into my possession tomorrow."

3.
[Sept. 18, 1958 – Quemoy]

A week after he received his assignment from Oscar Pendleton, Carter Hexam boarded a 17-year-old Curtiss C-46 Commando at Formosa's Taipei airport for the relatively short flight to Quemoy. He shared the cabin with a handful of passengers and several dozen cargo boxes, each bearing the emblem of the International Cooperation Administration, a U.S. State Department organization tasked with coordinating foreign assistance operations.

As fate would have it, another American accompanied him on the flight. Alex Garrett, a loquacious State Department minion, had been appointed to evaluate ICA services in Formosa to determine if additional aid might be warranted. Hexam immediately pegged him as an institutional greenhorn, most likely oblivious to the fact that all such missions had deeper political ramifications: Garrett's report would undoubtedly end up in the hands of the CIA for data collection purposes.

Despite the noisy drone of two powerful Wright Twin Cyclone engines, Garrett insisted on striking up a conversation with Hexam, though the OSP agent would have preferred silence.

"Long way from home," Garrett said after introducing himself. "What brings you here?"

"Photojournalist," Hexam said, pointing to the Leica MP camera strapped over his shoulder. He had used the cover story previously and did, on occasion, do freelance work for the specialty-press publications. "On assignment for *Bizarre Destinations* travel magazine."

"To Quemoy?" Garrett seemed perplexed. "Who would want to travel to Quemoy right now? It's under heavy shellfire from the mainland."

"That's the point," Hexam said. "*Bizarre Destinations* caters to people who want to see things they can't see at home – weird rituals, war zones, anything exotic or taboo."

"Fascinating." His vacant expression disclosed his lingering uncertainty. "I spend most of my vacations on the road with my family. We try to visit one or two National Parks each year."

"Very nice, I'm sure," Hexam said. He pictured Garrett with a bright, pretty, good-natured woman and a ragtag caravan of well-groomed, blonde-haired toddlers. "I'm sure they miss you when you're on assignment."

"Actually," Garrett said, glancing at their shared escort in his bucket seat across the cabin. Lt. Col. Feng

Chen-san of the Free Chinese Air Force paid no attention to either American. He spent most of the flight with his nose buried in a four-year-old copy of *Jungle Stories* – an issue of a pulp magazine he had acquired from Hexam back in Taipei. "This is my first trip abroad, Garrett admitted. "I'm as nervous as a kid on his first day of school."

"I'm sure you'll do fine."

"What about you? Family back home?"

"No," Hexam said, riled by the question. He never wore his wedding band while on assignment, and never discussed his family on the clock. "I avoid entanglements."

"Probably better in your line of work," Garrett said. "No one stateside worrying about you, no one for you to worry about when you're off roving around the world."

"Precisely," Hexam said, though his dedication to the charade wavered. Garrett had inadvertently struck a nerve: Hexam, as he grew older, found it more difficult to undertake missions that would keep him separated from his family for extended periods. "No need to get mired down in all that nonsense."

"I wouldn't mind tagging along with you once we arrive," Garrett said. "Tomorrow I'll be stuck in meetings and inventory sessions all day. I'd like to do a bit of sightseeing while I have a chance."

"Sorry, no can do." Hexam left little room for argument. "I'm on a tight schedule. A guide will be picking me up at the airport as soon as we land. Besides, I work better on my own."

Hexam's flat refusal quashed any further attempts at chitchat for the remainder of the flight. Garrett frittered away the minutes methodically reviewing his mission directives, scribbling marginalia on typewritten documents secured in a three-ring binder and nibbling on his fingernails. Lt. Col. Feng Chen-san occasionally peered over the top edge of *Jungle Stories,* offering an amiable smile to Hexam. His expression soured whenever he glanced at Garrett, betraying an inexplicable trace of animosity.

After a bumpy landing on a rutted airstrip, Hexam and Garrett followed their escort into a nearby Quonset hut. The sporadic thump of shellfire rumbled through the semicircular structure made out of corrugated galvanized steel. For the last month, the Reds had pounded the island, firing up to 55,000 high-explosive shells a day.

Only 13 miles long and eight miles across at its widest point, Quemoy was home to roughly 43,000 people. Much to Mao Zedong's consternation, the 50-square-mile island remained an outpost of Chiang Kai-shek's Kuomintang nearly a decade after the establishment of the People's Republic of China and the end of large-scale campaigns in the Chinese Civil War.

For the Reds, the island was a stepping stone to crushing the Kuomintang. For the Nationalists, it was a buffer and a potential staging area should Chiang Kai-shek ever manage to rally a sufficient army to invade the mainland. For the Americans, Quemoy had become yet another symbolic boundary in the fight to stop the spread of communism. In 1950, President Harry Truman clarified the stance when he said "the occupation of Formosa by Communist forces would be a direct threat to the security of the Pacific area and to United States forces performing their lawful and necessary functions in that area."

President Dwight D. Eisenhower upheld that doctrine.

To protect Formosa, the Seventh Fleet of the United States Navy – for the second time in less than a decade – gathered in the Formosa Straight packing considerable firepower. Hexam knew that the Air Force had prepared for a possible nuclear strike against Red China – but he doubted the current conflict would reach that level of aggression. In fact, he suspected that the current hostilities may have been sparked by the very thing he had been assigned to recover.

Hexam had been an integral part of the Office of Strategic Preservation since its founding in 1945. He knew the OSP generally avoided territorial disputes unless some component of the struggle warranted intervention. The agency initially restricted its activities to investigating reports of Soviet breakthroughs in pseudoscientific fields including extra-dimensional communication, remote viewing, cryptoarcheology, electrogravitics and psychokinesis. Since the early 1950s, the OSP had increasingly engaged in direct confrontation with what agency directors euphemistically termed "Invasive Entities."

According to Hexam's overseers, the object – a 12,000-year-old device crafted by alien refugees – would be smuggled off the mainland to Quemoy by an unnamed defector. If the artifact lived up to expectations, OSP involvement in Quemoy would be more than justified.

"Take a seat inside, Mr. Hexam," Chen-san said. His English was impeccable. Earlier, he had explained to Hexam that he went to school in England. "Your guide will be here momentarily. It was a pleasure meeting you." Chen-san next turned to the State Department agent. "Follow me, Mr. Garrett. We have some files you may find useful."

The two ventured deeper into the warehouse-sized Quonset hut, passing through a door set in a flimsy partition wall. A moment later, Hexam heard raised voices and what sounded like a struggle. Someone fired a pistol, its report nearly deafening in the enclosed space. Hexam stood, positioning himself behind a vacated desk, and kept one hand on his holstered Luger P08 automatic.

"My apologies, Mr. Hexam," Lt. Col. Feng Chen-san said, reappearing in the doorway. Two soldiers followed, dragging the limp body of Alex Garrett across the floor. "His papers turned out to be forged. Your intelligence bureau informed us as we were leaving Taipei. They say he's a Soviet agent, aligned with a group of Chinese cultists."

"The Tong of the Silver Shadow?"

"Precisely," Chen-san said, clearly impressed with Hexam's deduction.

"Any idea what he was doing here?"

"We do not ask those kinds of questions, Mr. Hexam." Chen-san grinned. He understood the cat-and-mouse games played by the world's two great ideological adversaries. "Besides, you probably already know the answer."

"What will happen to him?"

"He will be transferred into the custody of American military personnel back in Formosa," Chen-san said. "Your CIA will want to interrogate him."

"He seeks the Dropka stone," said a withered old Asian peasant wearing thick spectacles, a frock coat and wide trousers. He stepped timidly into the Quonset hut through the doorway and offered his hand reluctantly to Hexam. "I am Sun Jianying, at your services. Honor is mine," he said, his English not as seamless as Feng Chen-san's. He fished through his pockets searching for documents to prove his identity. "I come always from the Baian-Kara-Ula. I am keeper of the Elder Key, opener of all ancient doorways."

"The honor is mine," Hexam said affably as he inspected the old man's imperfect paperwork. Chen-san eyed the certificate over Hexam's shoulder, equally suspicious. "I was led to believe that you had not yet arrived on Quemoy," Hexam explained, sensing the man's discomfort. "How did you manage to elude the Red Army?"

"I show you – only you," Jianying said, an unsettling grin erupting across his otherwise grim features. "Come, quickly," he continued. "No time. We must be hurrying. There are others ..."

"One moment," Chen-san barked. "Exactly where do you plan to take Mr. Hexam?"

"Back," Jianying said, his expression conveying a rising level of apprehension. "Back to the Baian-Kara-Ula. Please, before other servants of the Silver Shadow are stopping us." He paused, perplexed by Hexam's unwillingness to take him at his word. Grudgingly, he thrust an arm into a leathern satchel at his side. From it, he plucked a flat jade disc, approximately 30 centimeters in diameter, with a circular hole at its center. "It is the Elder Key," Jianying said. "I must be keeping it safe. Come quickly, now."

Upon the face of the jade disc, two grooves originated from the hole in its center, forming a double spiral. Within each groove, Hexam could see intricate hieroglyph-like markings.

Hexam, recognizing the symbols upon the artifact, nodded in silent accord.

"Perhaps I should accompany you," Chen-san said. "I am supposed to ensure your safety on Quemoy. Also, I would like to see exactly how this gentlemen plans to transport you to the Baian-Kara-Ula."

"Considering the size of this island," Hexam said, "It shouldn't be difficult. How far is it?"

"The Baian-Kara-Ula is a branch of the Kunlun Mountains," Chen-san said. "The range runs through the Qinghai and Sichuan provinces of mainland China. I would estimate that the distance from here to there is approximately 2,300 kilometers."

* * *

Though Sun Jianying favored using his feet, Lt. Col. Feng Chen-san managed to persuade the defector to make the trip to the village of Chin-men-chiu-ch'eng in a jeep. The short trip gave Carter Hexam an opportunity to survey the damage wrought by the seemingly ceaseless Red artillery fire. Forests filled with healthy trees had been reduced to fields of jagged stumps. Acres of scenic, flat terrain had been scarred with shell craters. Villages had been flattened and island inhabitants killed, maimed and made homeless.

The thunder of artillery shells followed them all along their route as the Communist-held mainland continued to hammer the island with their biggest guns.

Arriving in the village, Jianying directed them to a centuries-old Buddhist Temple built into the side of Mount Taiwu.

"This way, this way," Jianying insisted, leaping from the still-moving jeep. He scrambled up the hillside nearly disappearing in the vegetation. "Hurry!"

Hexam lingered a few seconds, examining the once picturesque village. Though it sat upon the southeastern corner of the island, farthest from the mainland, the Reds still managed to reach it with their artillery. Hexam watched residents shambling through rubble and ruin, picking through heaps of broken brick and piles of splintered roof tiles.

"They are stronger than you think," Chen-san said, sensing Hexam's sympathy. "We are a very resilient race, Mr. Hexam. Many of the villagers have become cave dwellers, seeking refuge in tunnels in Mount Taiwu. They will survive this bombardment, no matter how long it takes the Americans to convince the mainland to silence their guns."

"I admire their courage," Hexam said. "But it troubles me that it has come to this. Even though the events of the world reach America, this kind of turmoil and havoc cannot be conveyed in newsprint or through summations uttered by radio and television journalists."

"There are many vigilant Americans, Mr. Hexam," Chen-san said. "Not everyone needs to know the smallest of details in each conflict."

"There is more to it than that, Lt. Col. Feng Chen-san – and I suspect you sense it, too." Carter Hexam – like his father and grandfather – possessed a keen instinct in certain matters – particularly incidents involving other-worldly forces that the Office of Strategic Preservation had been assigned to combat. "Chaos thrives in the most remote corners of the world. It flourishes in places where people are disheartened, exhausted, famished or desperate. Once entrenched, chaos always seeks to extend its potency and its sphere of influence."

"You speak of chaos as if it was itself an entity," Chen-san said.

"It is time," Jianying said, tugging on Hexam's sleeve. The old man led them into the ruined temple, over mounds of rubble and through strangely darkened rooms pierced by blinding beams of sunlight surging through gaping holes in the walls and ceiling. Approaching a smooth granite wall, Jianying pulled the jade disc from his satchel and placed it into a shallow, circular hollow in the stone. "We go now."

Jianying waited a moment before thrusting his fingers through the center hole of the disc. Chen-san and Hexam turned toward each other, their disbelief evident.

The shallowness of the hollow should not have allowed Jianying to do what he did. Jianying grasped the disc firmly and rotated it to the right.

Almost immediately, a doorway appeared in the granite. In that very instant, the crack of rifle fire echoed through the abandoned temple. Hexam's hand reflexively gripped his Luger as his gaze swept the shadows. He counted at least three snipers hiding in the debris.

"Go now," Jianying shouted, shepherding the two men through the doorway and into a dark, filthy, foul-smelling corridor. As the old Asian peasant retrieved the jade disc, a bullet struck him in the back, burrowing into his lungs. He stumbled forward as the doorway evaporated, coughing and moaning before collapsing to his knees. "Waste no time with me," Jianying said as Hexam eased him onto his side. "Take the Elder Key. Follow the passage, straight. You will be coming to a golden slab. Use the disc to open the door. Others will be helping," he said, faltering. He shuddered as waves of pain tortured his body and contorted his face. "Straight," he repeated, "in passage, do not leave it ... too much dangers in the abyss ... the Silver Shadow ..."

Life deserted the old man abruptly, his many secrets left unspoken.

Hexam resignedly retrieved the jade disc. Standing, he studied their surroundings.

"What is this place?" Chen-san – undoubtedly a man of courage and resolve, given his rank – could not help but betray a modicum of unease. His eyes sought the distant ceiling veiled in shadow and swept the broad and murky corridor bathed in an aberrant viridescent light. "It stinks of rotting human flesh – the smell of battlefield trenches filled with unattended corpses."

"I believe that this is a very ancient passageway," Hexam said, carefully selecting his words to explain the inexplicable. Hexam suspected that Jianying's doorway had transported them into an extra-dimensional domain – a potentially boundless, self-enclosed space constructed by the same aliens who forged the jade disc. "I suggest we follow the old man's instructions and see where this corridor leads."

Though Chen-san did not utter a word or show any sign of agreement, he followed as Hexam ventured deeper into the sinister sanctum of gargantuan pillars and indistinct arches and perpetually branching corridors. Like a subterranean charnel house, the place reeked of hoary death and decay and mold. Their feet plodded through turbid pools and over damp, slimy stone.

As they shambled halfheartedly down the gloomy passage, they passed by countless "hidden" doorways – each made evident only by a singular shallow, circular indentation. Each dimple contained a solitary identifying symbol, though without a map the pictograms had no meaning. Nevertheless, Hexam committed as many of these to memory as possible. The surfaces seemed solid enough to the touch, but Hexam found if he stared at the portals their faces rippled with indistinct, phantom shapes.

Slowly, as their eyes grew accustomed to the strange grue radiance, Hexam found the source of uncanny light far above the floor of the colossal walled labyrinth – but he dared not bring it to the attention of his companion. Overhead, faintly glowing stars – burning wearily in dreadful hues of yellow and green – presided over long-dead worlds in some wretched, blighted sector of the multiverse.

No more than an hour had passed when Hexam and Chen-san reached the ornate golden slab of which poor old Jianying had spoken. Hexam carefully placed the jade disc into place and rotated it slightly to the right. A doorway materialized, and the two men entered a remote, torch-lit cave carved into the side of a cliff somewhere in the Baian-Kara-Ula, deep in the Sichuan Province of mainland China.

If there remained any question regarding their whereabouts, a small contingent of Red Army soldiers welcomed the two men by pointing rifles at them.

4.

[Sept. 19, 1958 – Sichuan Province, People's Republic of China]

"This is unexpected," Carter Hexam said, glancing at his companion. In one hand, the OSP agent grasped the Elder Key. The fingers of his other hand hovered above his Luger P08 automatic. "Sorry to have gotten you involved in this minor debacle."

"Quite all right," said Lt. Col. Feng Chen-san, saluting the soldiers as he stepped away from the door. "I am afraid that I am responsible for orchestrating this ruse." He spat out a string of commands in Chinese before turning his attention back to Hexam. "I wonder if you would mind giving me the Elder Key."

Chaos.

Hexam felt its clever agents regulating every incident gleefully, pushing humanity toward the brink of pandemonium. With such a critical artifact in play, he knew even the closest allies could be compromised – and the most ruthless enemies could be driven to commit unspeakable atrocities.

"You could have taken it back in Quemoy," Hexam said, holding onto the jade disc stubbornly. "Why go to all this trouble ... unless – "

"Unless I did not know the location of the portal," Chen-san said. "Quite right. Had I known I could have secured that information from the Tong of the Silver Shadow, I would have rounded up their operatives months ago and had them tortured."

"You arranged this entire charade to locate the doorways," Hexam said, embarrassed that his government had not suspected duplicity. The Office of Strategic Preservation had been duped. "I warn you, Chen-san: The forces at work here are beyond anything you can imagine."

"The People's Republic of China is not interested in your counsel, Mr. Hexam," Chen-san said, no trace of clemency in his tone. "Now, I insist: Hand over the Elder Key."

"I'm afraid that won't be possible today, my treacherous friend," a clipped British voice said, its unrestrained confidence evoking a mental image of T.E. Lawrence. In reality, the speaker appeared far less handsome and agile and civilized. Stepping from a shadowed corner, the Englishman revealed himself as stout and stocky, with pasty skin, curly hair, a square face and bushy beard. "Sorry Chen-san: My squad of Tibetan expatriates relieved your soldiers an hour ago. Chin up, Hexam: These boys have no intention of pulling their triggers – unless I give them the signal."

"How considerate," Carter Hexam said, recognizing his British counterpart. He had worked with Ambrose Shelton on occasion – and certainly welcomed his intrusion given the situation, though he could not surmise how he managed to show up at precisely the right moment. "I can assure you that I will not give you any cause for concern, in that case. As for Chen-san ..."

As if taking a cue, Lt. Col. Feng Chen-san lunged toward Hexam, catching Shelton's entourage off guard. Hexam, however, anticipated the reckless assault and easily sidestepped the clumsy Red Army officer before bringing his pistol down hard against his skull. Chen-san grunted and staggered sideways, floundering as he tried to keep his balance. Before he could summon the energy for a second attack, Shelton barked a single word and the soldiers opened fire.

Chen-san slumped to the floor of the cave, his body riddled with bullets.

"Now that we've sorted that out," Shelton said, shaking Hexam's hand, "I must say I am pleased that your OSP chose you for this mission. It's quite a staggering find, wouldn't you say? Sun Jianying is as eager to share his knowledge with the West as he is fearful of what would happen if Mao Zedong claimed the Dropka stones." Shelton paused, his eyes growing glassy at the revelation of Jianying's absence became apparent. "Where is he? Where is Jianying?"

"Dead," Hexam said. "A victim of the Tong of the Silver Shadow, I believe."

"Those cretins." The Englishman shook his head in genuine disgust. "Possessing one stone is like stealing a key with no knowledge of what it unlocks."

"What about the Red Army?" Hexam feigned fatigue as he scrutinized the interior of the cave. Along one wall, he saw stacks of jade discs beneath crudely drawn maps. "Do they realize what these doorways really are?

"They have a limited understanding," the Englishman said. "From what I gather, they only wish to use it as a backdoor to Quemoy and other territories they seek to annex. They do not comprehend that there is a far greater reward. What did you think of your journey through the Domain of the Silver Shadow?"

"A convenient bypass, slipping in between parallel universes like that to travel thousands of miles in mere minutes," Hexam said. "Not a very hospitable environment. I would expect prolonged exposure to that milieu might have unfavorable effects on one's well-being."

"You're lucky you didn't get lost," the Englishman said, as if speaking from experience. "From what Sun Jianying taught me, that labyrinth is trillions of years old – older than our universe. The architects originally conceived of it as a kind of transdimensional hub, using it to colonize far-flung worlds and countless parallel universes."

"Later on it became a way to banish their adversaries," Hexam guessed. "Now it houses the scattered brethren of the Great Old Ones and Outer Gods – entities such as Azathoth, Tsathoggua and Cthulhu."

"There are far more unspeakable things hidden within those corridors than those trivial creatures," Shelton said, a tinge of fear darkening his eyes. "Old Jianying revealed as many secrets as he could, given his imperfect English. He was the last of them, you know – the last of the Dropka tribe entrusted with the stones."

Though Hexam held his tongue, Shelton's comment sparked a kernel of distrust. His intuition fluttered with hazy, inarticulate forewarnings.

Before Hexam had time to appraise the situation, a clatter arose, echoing through the narrow cavern.

"That would be the real Red Army," Shelton said. "The Communists must have heard the gunfire. It will only take them a few minutes to reach us." Shelton turned to Hexam, a sudden look of exasperation in his eyes. "We have to hurry. Help us gather the Dropka stones. Together, they comprise a map of the Domain of the Silver Shadow. Along with the Elder Key, they will allow us to explore the farthest reaches of the multiverse."

Hexam did as he was asked, but not before snapping several pictures of the crude map covering the cave wall. He hoped his Leica MP camera would capture the images efficiently despite the flickering torch light. As he carefully filled burlap sacks with the coveted jade discs, his eyes scoured the drawing searching for familiar symbols.

He stifled a smile as his gaze found one particular Olmec glyph.

Nearly an hour later, Hexam led Shelton and his Tibetan expatriates through the labyrinthine realm situated at the intersection of incalculable parallel universes. Above, the dying green and yellow stars emitted lurid light illuminating charred worlds speckled with the carcasses of extinct civilizations. A garish shadow, fuliginous in tint, hovered vigilantly over its vast domain, mindful of the passage of trespassers but mired in eternal apathy.

"Things could have gone quite differently if Chen-san had secured the Elder Key," Hexam said, his mind cycling over a number of scenarios. No matter how many times he evaluated Shelton's account, he kept coming up with too many unanswered questions. "Tell me, how did you manage to find Sun Jianying?"

"He found me," Shelton said. "I was working on a joint expedition with colleagues from Miskatonic University eight months ago, excavating ruins near Pagan in Burma. While working alone in an underground temple, Jianying appeared and told me his story. I didn't believe him – until I followed him into the Domain of the Silver Shadow."

"And he chose you as his successor," Hexam said, phrasing the comment so that it could be registered simultaneously as a question. "It seems curious that he would contact the Americans on Quemoy about defecting given that he had already found a suitable replacement."

"To a man like Sun Jianying, the British and the Americans are indistinguishable from one another," Shelton said. "I certainly had no qualms with bringing in the Yanks, so long as it was an OSP operation. As I mentioned, I'm glad they sent you, old chap."

"And you arrived at the right moment," Hexam said. "How did you know?"

"Jianying alerted me to your impending arrival."

"This is the door," Hexam said abruptly, holding out his hand. "Now listen: I expect the snipers who killed Jianying are still in the temple, waiting to ambush whoever comes through the portal. Shelton, instruct your men to advance quickly through the arched doorway into the antechamber, guns ready. Have them proceed to the exterior of the temple without delay, find cover and flush out the gunmen. Agreed?"

"Agreed," Shelton said, turning to translate the directions to his soldiers. "Ready."

"Ready," Hexam repeated, using the Elder Key to open the portal. Immediately, the Tibetan expatriates dashed through the room and into the darkness beyond. "Help me haul the Dropka stones into the chamber while we wait."

Having deposited hundreds of jade discs in a chamber he considered unapproachable, Hexam turned toward Shelton, the Luger P08 automatic trained on the traitor.

"This is not Quemoy," Hexam said calmly. "We are in the Temple of the Feathered Serpent near Cobata, Mexico, currently under the supervision of the OSP. Your friends are either dead or in custody. The lack of gunfire suggests they surrendered. I suggest you do likewise."

"I don't understand," Shelton stuttered. "I arranged all of this."

"Jianying did not trust you enough to bring you to Quemoy," Hexam said. "And from comments he made, I believe other members of the Dropka tribe were alive when he traversed the Domain of the Silver Shadow. What became of them remains to be seen," Hexam said with a hint of disgust. "When my fellow agents arrive, they will want to know when you became a free agent … and who tipped you off that I was arriving in Quemoy."

5.
[Sept. 27, 1958 – Tokyo]

On a rutted road in a suburban Tokyo neighborhood, beneath a streetlamp outside a charming little inn not far from the Sumida River, a tall, hard-faced American lit a Cuban cigar. His co-conspirator arrived at the rendezvous several minutes late and offered an adequate excuse.

"The Brit was shot down, I'm told." The American scowled as he delivered the news. "The Americans have the Elder Key."

"We moved too sluggishly," his acquaintance said, his Russian accent too thick to conceal. "Our man should have intercepted him."

"We will have other opportunities," the American said. "Tomorrow is another day."

Two shots rang out in rapid succession, momentarily disrupting the late-night tranquility. Each figure slumped to the ground gracefully, lifeless.

Hexam allowed himself a wry smile.

Order had been restored.

www.ingramcontent.com/pod-product-compliance
Lightning Source LLC
LaVergne TN
LVHW012020060526
838201LV00061B/4383